CORSONIA

Praise for Susan Berliner's novels:

The Disappearance

"*The Disappearance* is a terrific read...gratifying and suspenseful...for both young adults as well as adults. I highly recommend *The Disappearance*. Its message is thought-provoking and one young adults must keep in mind as they mature into adulthood." — *Night Owl Reviews (Top Pick)*

"I enjoy reading books with time travel - and this book took you back and forth constantly! It was done in such a way that had me almost believing it was really possible." — Michele Bodenheimer, *Miki's Hope*

"There are many modes of time travel, but this one takes the cake - so different from others I've read! Whatta way to travel - makes me slightly dizzy. This group of characters working together to bring down one culprit is so different, so eclectic; it's a wonder they ever met each other! But that's what makes it work! I love 'The Sting' all over again." — Lila L. Pinord

"I just loved this book! This is one of those books that will call you to pick it back up if you have the self-control to set it down for a moment. I was pulled in throughout the entire story because I could not wait to see what would happen next." — Dawn Fitzpatrick

Peachwood Lake

"It is a marvelous coming of age horror story." — *Night Owl Reviews (Top Pick)*

"*Peachwood Lake* is another winner for new author Susan Berliner...Where else are you going to find a fish horror story that brings a young girl's life into focus?...I have no trouble recommending this book for the pre-teen/YA horror lover. Five out of five fairy kisses for this reader." — Dottie Taylor, *Tink's Place*

"Great read. Fun and suspenseful. Best fish story since *Jaws*!" — Peggy Derevlany

"This author creates characters with many layers and creatures that are so different from the average thriller type read that I can't wait to see what she comes up with next!" — Paula Davis

"I absolutely LOVED it! I can see this being a movie, a very awesome movie!" — Heather Marts

Dust

"Susan Berliner gives us an amazing mysterious supernatural story in
Dust. It intrigues and holds the readers' attention, while pulling them in
and not letting them put it down."   *– Night Owl Reviews (Top Pick)*

"*Dust* picks you up and takes you on a whirlwind ride, pun intended,
and doesn't let you go until the final climax...It's a great piece of escapist
fiction and a book to easily get lost in."   – Patricia Lane

"Susan Berliner's first novel is filled with drama, laughter, and engaging
characters...As a high school English teacher, I plan to use this
captivating novel with my students this year. I give *DUST* an A+!"
                                                            – Brittany Mott

"I was able to read this book in its entirety within just a few hours, which
added to its cinematic qualities; it was like watching a movie in the
afternoon...The language in the book is relatively simple and casual, easy
to read, and doesn't contain much in the way of profanity, so it can be
enjoyed by a wide age-group spectrum."   – Andy S. Adams

CORSONIA

by Susan Berliner

Published by SRB Books

ISBN: 978-0-9839401-4-2

Cover design by Book Graphics
Book layout by Dianne Paulet
Author's photo by Rachel Leib Photography

Published December, 2014

Printed in the United States of America

Dedicated to the memory of my parents,
Olga and Joseph Wettenstein,
who supported everything I did,
good and bad,
from creative writing to playing the violin.

Thanks to David and Merri,
Lisanne Harrington and Eddie Estupinan
for their invaluable input,
which improved this novel.
And special thanks to my husband, Larry,
who always does all he can
to help me succeed.

"That which consumes your mind,
controls your life."
—Anonymous

CHAPTER 1

"Just one more picture!" Loren Cofton begged.

Tracie Martinez stuck out her tongue at her friend and shook her head vigorously.

"No. You've taken enough. There's absolutely nothing here to photograph. What're you gonna tell everyone? That this is a ghost town called Delano, Nevada and it used to have a gold mine, it used to have buildings, it used to..."

"Okay, okay, I get it," Loren said, moving away from the brush and slipping the smartphone into her jeans pocket. "I just figured people could imagine what was here a hundred years ago and then make a story out of it. Wouldn't that be cool?"

"I guess." Tracie shrugged as she began walking to the Prius parked nearby on the rutted dirt road. "I'm glad you're finally ready to go 'cause it feels like it's a hundred degrees, even though it's already after four. I want to be at our motel before it gets dark, just in case we have trouble finding it."

"How could we have any trouble?" Loren asked. "You're good with directions, we've got the GPS, and it's not like you have to check address numbers here." She waved her hand at the desolate landscape. "There're no houses or anything and we haven't even seen another car since we turned onto this tiny road."

"Well, maybe there'll be houses and people and stores further along the way to the motel," Tracie said, glancing left and then right. "Anyway, this place is starting to give me the creeps."

"Boo!" Loren shouted as she jumped into the driver's seat, turned on the ignition, and immediately switched on the air conditioning. "I just want to see a food store. All this heat is making me real thirsty and I finished the last bottle of water."

"I hope this is it with the stupid ghost towns," Tracie said as Loren drove south on the deserted mountain road toward Montello.

"Well, there's one more somewhere around here that Wikipedia said had a bunch of buildings still standing."

Tracie threw her head back on the seat and groaned.

"It'll be fun," Loren continued. "We can look at the mine entrances and maybe find stuff that the miners used and then dumped. You know, artifacts."

"It's been too many years, Lor. There's nothing left from them anymore. Swimming in the Great Salt Lake yesterday was so much better—and cooler. Just how many more of these dumb, boring places do we have to see till you've finally had enough?"

"I don't know. I still keep hoping to find something good...Hey what's this?" Loren swung off the road onto the gravel shoulder, put the car in reverse, and backed up several feet. "Look, Trace. There's another little road here. I wonder where it leads."

"You know exactly where it leads—to nowhere. There's absolutely nothing on or off County Road 766 or even 765—that's what the GPS says, that's what the maps say, that's what everything and everybody says." Tracie glanced at the map of Elko Country on her lap. "When we get to Route 233 by the motel there'll be people and places, but not here."

"It won't take long to check this out though," Loren said as she turned onto the narrow paved strip. "It's still a road so there could be something, maybe even a store selling drinks. I'm really thirsty."

Loren drove along the small road for nearly a mile as her friend continued to complain. "See," Tracie muttered. "It's just like I said. Nothing's here except more bushes and rocks."

Then, without any warning, the landscape changed and they approached a large clearing with several buildings on both sides. "Aha!" Loren shouted. "I was right. A road always leads to something and this looks a lot like a shopping center, which means there's a town." After turning off the ignition, she smirked at Tracie. "So what do you say now?"

Tracie studied the open map once again and shook her head. "There's nothing in here about any town and I just bought this map yesterday."

Loren waved her arm at the group of buildings. "Well, this is definitely something so let's check it out."

The two girls stepped out of the car into the late afternoon heat. "This place looks deserted and I'm getting the creeps again," Tracie said as she wiped beads of sweat from her forehead. "I don't see any other cars or people and all these buildings look like they're empty. Let's get out of here."

"Maybe it's another ghost town, one that's not on any map," Loren said, retrieving her smartphone. "Then we can discover it and post the video on YouTube." She started filming the vacant road and the surrounding buildings.

"You got ten minutes starting now," Tracie said, checking her watch as they headed toward a beige stone structure. "Then we leave."

Loren ignored her friend's words as they reached the building.

"This one's a bank," Tracie said, pointing to the sign's engraved lettering. "Commerce Bank of Nevada." Taking a tissue from her jeans pocket, she wiped the dirt-encrusted windows and tried to see inside. "But it doesn't look old enough to be part of a ghost town. There're counters and posters on the wall and the floor's tiled. Everything seems in good shape."

"So then maybe the bank just closed suddenly and some other buildings here are still open," Loren said as she stuffed the phone back in her pocket. "Damn! I was hoping to discover a new ghost town."

Tracie walked to the building next to the bank and again attempted to peer through the windows. "This one looks empty and clean too. There's no store sign, but I think it was a hair salon. I can see chairs, mirrors, and couple of hair dryers and sinks in the back."

"Let's check the other side of the street," Loren suggested. "Damn, it's hot here."

The two girls stepped into the dusty road and headed for the nearest building, a red brick structure. Halfway across, Loren put her hand on her friend's arm. "Did you hear that?" she asked, pointing toward the far right. "I heard something over there."

"It sounds like some kind of machine," Tracie said as the girls rushed toward the source of the noise.

"I don't know what it is," Loren called, zipping past her friend. "But it sure sounds like it's being made by a person and that means there's something happening here."

The squeaking noise emanated from a store at the end of the small shopping center. When Tracie reached the building, which the overhead sign identified as "Phil's Food Mart," Loren was already tugging at the front door.

"It's locked," Loren said. "But the sound's coming from the back so someone's gotta be working there."

The girls dashed to the rear of the building where a heavily bearded man in his fifties, his long brown hair in a ponytail, wheeled a squeaky cart filled with 16-ounce unlabeled bottles of water through the back door of the store. Inside, cartons of the same bottles covered most of the floor.

"Yes!" Loren shouted. "We are saved!" She beamed proudly at her friend. "See how good it was that we checked this place out?"

"Okay, okay," Tracie said. "So you were right this time. Now stop gloating and let's get a couple of waters and then leave. I'm hot as hell." She shook her sweaty tee shirt with both hands, trying to fan herself.

As the girls talked, the man with the cart ignored them completely and continued to wheel cases of plastic bottles from a rusted blue pickup truck into the store.

"Excuse me," Loren said, stepping into the doorway. "Could we please buy two bottles of water? How much do they cost?"

The man stopped unloading the cart and turned toward the girls. He stood without moving and didn't speak.

"I asked if we could buy two bottles," Loren repeated. "We're both really thirsty."

Although the man continued to face the girls, he stared straight ahead, seeming to focus on something past them.

Tracie grabbed Loren's hand and tried to pull her away. "Come on," she whispered. "Let's just go." But her friend didn't budge.

"This water is not for you," the longhaired bearded man finally said, still standing motionless and gazing into the distance. "You cannot drink it." He pronounced each word slowly and carefully, speaking in a monotone, without any inflection in his voice.

"Okay, sir," Tracie said, still tugging on Loren's hand. "Thank you. We understand. Your water's not for sale. Sorry to have bothered you, but we're leaving now."

"Yeah," Loren echoed, releasing her hand from Tracie's grip as they both took several steps backwards, turned, and walked away.

The man nodded once and entered the store. As soon as he was out of sight, Loren dashed to the truck and grabbed a bottle.

"What did you just do?" Tracie asked when Loren caught up

with her and they continued toward the car.

"I just took this," Loren said, showing her friend the water.

"You stole a bottle!"

"Yeah. So you think that guy'll come back and arrest me?"

Tracie shuddered. "He was really creepy. It was weird the way he talked and he didn't look at us at all."

"Like some kind of robot man," Loren agreed, rotating the bottle of water in her hand. "Wonder why he wouldn't sell this to us. I mean it's just water. Doesn't even have a label or anything on it."

"Maybe it's well water from someplace around here," Tracie suggested. "And that's why he said we shouldn't drink it." She put her hand on the other girl's arm. "Lor, maybe this water's got extra minerals in it that'll make you sick. Throw it away. We'll be at the motel in less than an hour and then you can get all the water you want."

"Nah. I'm too thirsty." Loren reached into her small shoulder bag, took out the car keys, and tossed them to Tracie. "Here. You drive. You know the way to the motel. I'm just gonna lean back, relax, and drink my stolen water."

"Ah," Loren sighed, twisting open the bottle as Tracie began driving to Montello. "Kinda warm, clear, clean water. Want some?" She shoved the bottle in front of Tracie's face.

"No. I'll wait till we get to the motel. You should wait too, but you won't listen to me anyway so go ahead and do what you want."

"Okay. If you insist." Loren lifted the bottle to her mouth and took a large swallow. "Very good," she said. "Maybe it has extra minerals and stuff, but it tastes real refreshing." She hoisted the bottle to her mouth again. "Sure you don't want any? 'Cause otherwise I'm gonna finish it."

Tracie shook her head.

"Then here goes." Loren quickly drank the rest of the water and tossed the empty bottle on the backseat floor. "Umm, I'm real sleepy now. Gonna rest for a while." She leaned her head against the seat and closed her eyes.

"Go ahead," Tracie said, checking the GPS. "We've still got a ways to go so I'll wake you when we get there." She turned on the car radio, but after getting only static and no stations, she inserted a Beatles' CD—something an awake Loren would never have allowed—lowered the volume and listened to the music as she drove.

Tracie made a sharp left onto County Road 765, another tiny route with no traffic. *Not exactly the LIE*, she thought, smiling as she envisioned her hometown Long Island, New York thoroughfare, notorious for its congestion.

"We're here!" Tracie announced as she pulled into the small parking lot of the Montello Inn. "Time to wake up now!"

Loren didn't respond.

"Hey, girl, I know I said you could take a nap, but we're at the motel so c'mon and get your tired ass up." Tracie reached over to the passenger seat and shook her sleeping friend.

Loren keeled further to the side, but didn't open her eyes.

Tracie unsnapped the girl's seat belt and stared at her unresponsive passenger, whose head now rested awkwardly against the door. She was breathing steadily and appeared to be in a deep sleep.

"Loren?" Tracie shook her friend again. "You've got to get up now. Please. You're scaring me."

But Loren didn't move. She continued to lean against the door with her eyes closed.

"Oh my God!" Tracie shouted. "What the hell was in that water?"

CHAPTER 2

Tracie burst into the motel's office and raced to the counter. "I need help!" she yelled.

"Calm down, miss," the pudgy middle-aged man seated behind the enclosure said as he rose to face her. "What's wrong?"

Tracie spoke quickly, without pausing for a breath. "It's my friend. She's sleeping in the car and I can't wake her up. She drank a bottle of water and said she was taking a nap, but now she won't get up. She needs a doctor. Do you know where can I get one fast?"

"Let's go outside first and look at your friend," the man said, stepping into the small lobby and smiling at Tracie. "Don't worry. It'll be okay."

"How can you say that?" Tracie shouted. "She's like in a coma. That's not normal sleeping."

"You said something about her drinking a bottle of water. Where'd she get it?"

"We stopped at this place off County Road 766 that looked like it was a shopping center, but all the buildings were closed. Then we saw a man in the back of a store that had lots of bottles of water and we asked if we could buy some and he said 'no.'" Tracie stared sheepishly at the desk clerk. "But my friend was thirsty so she took one anyway and drank it."

The man nodded, but said nothing.

When they reached the car, the man opened the passenger door, crawled inside, looked at the sleeping girl, and felt her pulse. "She's in a deep sleep all right," he said, backing out.

"So can you get a doctor or should I just take her to the emergency room of the hospital?"

The man shook his head. "Nah," he said. "You don't need no doctor for your friend. I've seen this happen before." He reached into the car, lifted Loren, and draped her over his shoulder.

"What do you mean?" Tracie asked as the man carried the sleeping girl into the motel's lobby.

"You girls was in Corsonia," he said, lowering Loren into one of the two armchairs. "That's the problem."

Tracie gave the man a puzzled look. "I don't understand," she said.

"Didn't the guy there say not to drink the water?"

"Yeah. What's the matter with it?"

The man shrugged. "I got no idea. But no one can drink that water unless they live in that town and the people there are real weird. They do their own thing."

"He talked funny and didn't look at us," Tracie said, nodding.

"We call Corsonia, 'Hippy Town.' Them people all live together and don't have nothin' to do with any other folks. The men all got long hair and beards. It's like the communes that they used to have back in the sixties—flower power, drugs, and that kind of thing. Probably share wives and kids too. We're right near the Utah border so that sort of stuff happens."

"You mean polygamy, like with Mormons?"

"Can't say for sure," the man said, shrugging again. "But we don't mess with any of them from Corsonia—and we know not to drink their water. Puts you to sleep."

Tracie walked to the armchair and lifted Loren's limp arm, rubbing it tenderly. "You said she doesn't need a doctor. When will she wake up?"

"Sometime tomorrow. Can't tell you the exact time, just that she's gonna be okay after that and there's nothing you can do now but just wait and let her sleep." He pointed to the door. "I'll help you bring in your gear and then we'll get your friend to the room so she'll be more comfy."

Tracie sat in the chair of the cozy motel room and stared at Loren, who lay in one of the twin beds, continuing her Sleeping Beauty-like slumber.

What the hell am I supposed to do now? she wondered as she dug into her shoulder bag and took out her phone, debating whether or not to call Loren's mother. *So then what do I tell her, that her daughter's in some kind of deep fairy-tale sleep?* Tracie leaned against the flowery upholstered chair, shaking her head. *I really screwed up.* She tossed the phone into the bag, closed her eyes, and tried to come up with a plan.

Tracie was supposed to be the sensible one, the person who would protect Loren and thwart her recklessness. In fact, that's why she was on this cross-country journey. True, she was the girl's best friend—and one of her few "real" friends—since most of their schoolmates were envious of Loren's wealth and only pretended to like her.

Even the boys were intimidated by Loren's overbearing father—a self-made millionaire who owned Chickyums, a local fast-food chain—and, although Loren was a pretty blonde, she had trouble sustaining relationships. At the end of the semester, she had broken up with her most recent boyfriend. So when Loren got a new Prius as a high school graduation present, it wasn't surprising that she had immediately decided to road test it on a lengthy car trip and asked Tracie to come along.

At first, Tracie had refused the invitation. The eldest of three children of a school janitor and a housecleaner, both Puerto Rican immigrants, she was poorer than most of her classmates and couldn't afford to go on a long summer vacation—even with Loren covering all their expenses—because she had to earn money for college. She had already lined up a decent-paying sales job at the local Macy's. But Loren wanted Tracie on the road trip and Loren's mom wouldn't let her only child travel alone. Mrs. Cofton begged Tracie to accompany Loren and when Tracie explained her financial situation, the woman said she would pay Tracie the same amount she'd be earning at Macy's so that, without taxes, she'd actually be making more.

Tracie wasn't sure if Loren knew she was being paid for this vacation. *Not really a spy*, she thought, squirming in the chair. But she did phone Mrs. Cofton about once a week. Loren's mom hadn't asked her to do so, but the woman seemed to appreciate the calls since her daughter rarely bothered to check in. And Tracie continued to feel uncomfortable not discussing her monetary arrangement with her friend.

So what now? She opened her eyes and scanned the small floral-decorated room. Tracie licked her lips, which felt very dry and chapped, and remembered how thirsty she was from spending the day in the hot sun. Her stomach was rumbling too. After a quick gaze at her sleeping companion, she jumped onto the unoccupied twin bed, picked up the phone on the end table, and hit the "O" button for the front desk.

The man who had helped her earlier answered the call. "Hello, miss," he said. "What can I do for you?"

"Can I get something to eat and drink brought to the room?" Tracie asked. "I don't want to go out and leave my friend here by herself in case she wakes up."

"She'll be sleeping for a while, I'm sure, but I can order food for you from the grill down the road. What do you want?"

"A burger, fries, and three bottles of water would be great. Thanks a lot."

"No problem," the motel clerk said. "I'll call it in right now. Shouldn't take too long."

"Thanks." Tracie hung up the phone. Then, after glancing at Loren again, she grabbed the remote and switched on the TV.

"Hey, Trace, where are we?"

The sound of Loren's sleep-slurred voice immediately woke Tracie, who sat up in bed and beamed at her friend. "Welcome back," she said.

"What d'ya mean?" Loren asked, rubbing her eyes. "How long have I been asleep? I don't remember anything since you started driving to the motel."

Tracie checked the clock-radio on the night table. "It's just after seven o'clock Wednesday morning," she said. "You've been out since about five yesterday afternoon."

"Wow!" Loren jumped up. "What the hell happened to me? I drank that bottle of water and got so sleepy."

"It was the water. Remember, the creepy man in that empty shopping center told us not to drink it and then the man in the motel here said no one except the people who live in that town can drink the water. Everyone else falls into a long deep sleep. I couldn't wake you up."

"That's impossible." Loren shook her head.

"It's some kind of weird place called Corsonia. The guy we saw there was weird and the people all live together in a commune and they don't do anything with anyone else. All the men have long hair and beards like the one we saw. The motel man called them hippies."

"Like flower children, LSD, peace?"

"I guess." Tracie shrugged, walked to Loren's bed, and gave her friend a quick hug. "I'm just glad you're okay 'cause you scared the shit out of me. Now let's get ready and go find a place to have breakfast. You must be starving because you haven't eaten since lunch yesterday. Then after, we can get out of here, start heading to California."

"Yeah," Loren agreed, standing up. "I am hungry. But after we eat, we're gonna stick around here for a while. That weird town's more interesting than anywhere else we've been or anything we'll see in California. I want to go back to that town and find out what's going on."

Tracie stared at her friend in shock. "You can't be serious," she whispered.

"Why not? I want to find out what was in that water. Do you still have the bottle I drank?"

"You threw it in the back after you finished it, but there's no water left."

"Well, maybe scientists can still analyze the bottle, find out what was in it that made me fall asleep."

"And where're we gonna find these scientists, Lor? We're in a tiny town in the middle of nowhere."

Loren studied the plain white ceiling before replying. "Then we'll just have to check this out by ourselves, play detective so we can figure out what happened to me." She smiled at her friend. "I've always wanted to know what a commune's like."

"No!" Tracie shook her head back and forth vigorously. "We can't do this. It's much too dangerous!"

"Okay. Then you can go home. I'll use my Mom's credit card and get you all the cash you need. There's gotta be a bus or a train somewhere around here you can take to an airport."

"Loren!" Tracie shouted. "You know I won't do that and leave you here by yourself!"

Again Loren smiled sweetly. "Then go get dressed so we can have breakfast and work out what we're gonna do next."

CHAPTER 3

Tracie found herself in a car speeding along the same empty road she had taken the previous day. Only this time, she was the passenger.

"This is gonna be a great adventure," Loren gushed as she drove north toward Corsonia, seemingly completely recovered from her lengthy sleep.

"These people don't want us there," Tracie said. "You heard that creepy man in the store. Did he sound like he wanted to make new friends?"

"That's only one person—and he didn't tell us to go away."

"He certainly didn't tell us to come back!"

Loren chuckled. "Trace, you're my BFF and I love you, but you've got no pioneer spirit. If you were around when Columbus wanted to sail to America, you would have told him to stay home. 'It's much too dangerous,'" she chided in a sing-song voice.

Tracie folded her arms and bit her lower lip, but said nothing.

"Don't you think it'll be fun seeing how people in a commune live?" Loren continued.

"If these people live in a commune by themselves, away from

everyone else, they sure don't want us hanging around. Besides, how are we going to find them? There was nothing open in the town and the motel guy didn't know how to get in touch with them. You didn't even find anything about the commune online."

"Yeah," Loren said. "That makes it even better. It means we just have to go back to the stores and look around some more—and this time we don't need their water." She tilted her head toward the floor of the backseat, which held the twelve-pack of bottles she had bought in a small convenience store near their motel.

Loren turned into the little unnamed road she had found the previous day and drove nearly a mile until they again reached the small shopping center. After switching off the car, she smiled at her friend. "We're here."

"It's just as empty as yesterday," Tracie said, her arms still folded. "No cars, no people, no open stores, no anything. This is a dumb idea."

"Maybe. But even if you don't like it, it's too hot to just sit in the car and wait for me." Loren opened the door, stepped outside, and glanced in all directions.

"Looks quiet," Loren said when Tracie finally joined her. "Let's check around again and see if we find anything new."

"There's nothing here," Tracie mumbled as they crossed the deserted street and walked toward the store at the far end of the center where they had seen the man.

The girls reached Phil's Food Mart, which was still closed, and headed to the back of the store. Loren tugged on the rear door, but it was locked.

"Like I said, nothing's here," Tracie repeated. "Not even that creepy man unloading his truck with the weird water that put you to sleep."

"But he was working here yesterday so there's gotta be something going on in this little town," Loren said. "C'mon. Let's get back into the car and continue down the road and see if we can find some people in houses."

"And if we do, you think they're gonna want to talk to you?"

"We won't know until we try," Loren said, smiling.

Loren drove slowly along the small road, which again was flanked by bushes, trees, and rolling hills. "There's gotta be something here," she complained. "Maybe I should stop and we can try walking past the bushes."

"What will that do? Without a road, there can't be cars so there won't be any people. You think they're living in tents outdoors in the meadows or maybe in caves?"

Loren shook her head. "I don't know where the people are. This doesn't make any sense."

"Let's go back to the motel, Lor, pack up, drive to Lake Tahoe and then on to California. Disneyland's supposed to be great and Universal..."

"We can do that sightseeing stuff any time," Loren cut in. "This is something different. Look! A house!" She stopped the car and pointed to a one-story building about fifty feet to the left of the road. "C'mon. Let's check it out."

Loren raced out of the car and rushed toward the small dwelling. Tracie followed, moving slowly.

"So?" Tracie asked when she reached Loren, who stood at the entrance.

"No one home," Loren said. "I already rang the bell and banged on the door."

"What a surprise—an empty house in this empty town. I bet this place is deserted too." Tracie wandered to the side of the building and peeked through a window. "Yup," she said. "I'm right, of course. No one's lived here in a long time. Windows are filthy and there're newspapers all over the floor."

Tracie continued sideways to the garage. "There's a car inside, but the driveway's a mess. It looks like it hasn't been used in years and there's not even a lawn, just lots of tall grass and weeds. Anyway, the man at the motel said the people here lived in a commune so they'd all be together somewhere, not in this little house."

"But the house's not empty," Loren said. "There's furniture in the living room—a sofa and tables and lamps." She stopped staring in the window and turned toward Tracie. "Why would people just move out and leave their car and all their stuff here?"

Tracie shrugged. "I don't know. Maybe they're not allowed to bring their things with them in a commune. You know, like starting new."

"I guess," Loren said, shaking her head. "I could never leave all my stuff like that. It's a crazy way to live."

"What now?" Tracie asked. "Are you finished here?"

"Yeah. Let's go back to the car and I'll figure out what we're gonna do next."

"I can hardly wait," Tracie mumbled.

"They've gotta be living somewhere," Loren said as she maneuvered into the bushes to turn the car and began driving back to CR-766. "Maybe there's another little road around here that we missed."

"I don't think we could've missed anything," Tracie said. "This town is so small."

"Well, even the guy at the motel told you there were people around here—and I intend to find them." As Loren drove past the deserted stores, a black SUV, heading in the opposite direction, pulled up in front of them, effectively blocking the tiny road.

A short squat man, wearing a cowboy hat, quickly stepped out of the car and walked to Loren's window. "Mornin', ladies," he said, lifting his Stetson and revealing a bald spot. "You two gals get lost?" He leaned closer to the window and smiled.

"Hi," Loren said, opening the window and returning the man's smile. "No. We're not lost. Actually, we were looking for the people who live in this town."

"Oh." The man stopped smiling and stared at the girl. "Why's that?"

"We heard they live in a commune and we were interested in finding out what that's like," Loren explained.

"I see." The man stood up and nodded his head several times before speaking. "Well, here's the problem," he began. "The folks who live in this place don't much like visitors." Reaching into his pants pocket, he took out a badge, which he thrust in front of Loren's face.

"I'm the elected sheriff of this little town and it's my job to do what the people here want me to do—and they tell me they don't like folks snooping around into their business." He tossed the badge into his pocket and poked his head inside the window. "Hope you both understand what I'm saying and will respect the feelings of the people who live here," he said, smiling once again. "I'd hate to have to arrest you two girls for unlawful entry." He reached into his holster and pulled out a gun, which he aimed at each girl's face.

"That's okay, officer," Tracie said quickly. "We're leaving right now."

"Good idea," the man said, continuing to smile sweetly at Loren and Tracie. "I knew a couple of smart girls like you would understand."

"Now that was a lot of fun," Tracie said as Loren continued driving toward CR-766. "And why'd you open your window to talk to that man? You didn't know who he was. He could've been an axe murderer."

"But he was a cop so it was okay."

"You didn't know that when you opened the window! Lor, he cut us off and he wasn't in a police car. The guy could've been a killer. Then no one would have even found our bodies." Tracie frowned at her friend. "So are you finished now? That sheriff warned us to stay away. Like I said—and he said—the people who live here don't want us around."

"Just because he told us that, doesn't mean it's true. We'll just have to try to find them another way." Loren grinned at Tracie. "I've always wanted to go for a hike in the Nevada hills so I'm gonna go to the motel, get my backpack, and come back here for a little afternoon hike—and maybe I'll accidentally find that commune."

"No!"

"Hey, Trace, if you don't want to come with me, you can still go home or just wait for me in the motel."

"You know I can't do that!"

Loren shrugged. "It's up to you, but I'm coming back here. That sheriff got real nervous when he found out we were looking for the people in that commune and he was just trying to scare us away. I'm sure there's no law against 'snooping around.' He can't arrest us for just walking in this town."

"He can arrest us for anything he wants. Who's going to know?"

"There's something strange going on here," Loren said. "I can feel it. That weird man and the water yesterday and now this sheriff who wants us to leave. But I'm gonna figure out what's happening."

Tracie leaned back in the seat and sighed. "So what's your plan?"

CHAPTER 4

"Here's where I'm gonna stop," Loren said Wednesday afternoon as she bounced the Prius off the county road, avoiding the scrubby bushes. "It looks like there used to be a road right here and someone covered it up with pebbles."

"Why would anyone do that?" Tracie asked.

"I don't know yet."

Loren parked behind a formation of rocky hills. "This'll hide us from anyone driving by," she said, turning off the car and stepping outside.

"Do you have enough water?" Tracie asked as she joined Loren.

"Three bottles."

"I took two. Hope that'll do it." Tracie looked overhead and adjusted her backpack. "The sun's real hot again this afternoon and we're sure not gonna drink any of the local brand."

"We shouldn't have to walk very far," Loren said. "The way I figure, we've just gotta hike past that next group of hills." She pointed to a connected series of large cliffs on their right. "If I wanted to hide somewhere around here, that's where I'd go—behind those rocks."

"Well, these people might not think like you."

"Yeah, but it's a small town and the commune's gotta be near those stores—and we're less than a half mile from that road."

"Okay," Tracie said. "I'm burning up just standing here. Let's go."

Loren and Tracie walked for more than ten minutes until they reached the barrier hills comprised of tall rocks with raggedy bushes sticking out like unruly hair. "Sorry," Loren said as she leaned against the stone, grabbed a bottle, and gulped the water. "That took longer than I thought."

"Yeah, and with the sun beating down on us the whole time." Tracie collapsed onto the pebble-filled ground. "And then we're gonna have to walk all the way back."

"C'mon." Loren grabbed her friend's arm. "Get up and let's see if I was right about houses hidden behind these rocks."

"Okay, okay," Tracie mumbled as she brushed the dirt off her rear end and followed Loren.

Although the mountainous rocks were intertwined, there were gaps between them and the girls maneuvered through one of the larger openings until they reached the other side.

"There!" Loren pointed triumphantly at several houses in the distance. "I told you!" Outside one of the buildings, shirts and pants flapped on a clothesline strung between two trees. "This place isn't empty. People are definitely living here so let's go and meet them."

"Hold on." Tracie grasped Loren's shoulder. "We can't just go over and knock on those people's doors and introduce ourselves. What if they get mad and tell the sheriff on us?"

"Yeah. Maybe you're right and we should be a little careful. Let's walk closer and figure out the best way to do this. Maybe we'll just watch first. What do you think?"

Tracie stared at Loren. "I can't believe you're actually listening to me and asking for my opinion. How come?"

"Well, I don't want these people to chase us away. If that happens, we'll never find out what's going on here. We need them to be our friends."

"I don't need friends like that creepy man by the store or the sheriff," Tracie said, shaking her head. "But we've come this far so we might as well finish this." She and Loren continued walking toward the cluster of houses.

The girls reached the first home and hid behind a small tree while they studied the house.

"What do you think?" Loren asked.

"I know there's laundry hanging behind one of these houses, but I don't think anyone's at home in this one," Tracie said. "There's no noise, no talking, no people, no cars..."

"Yeah," Loren agreed. "It's creepy again. But there's a dirt road over there so something's going on."

"Not much."

Loren stepped away from the tree. "I'm gonna take a chance and look in the window," she called as she ran to the house.

"I knew it wouldn't last," Tracie murmured, rolling her eyes as she slowly followed her friend. "So do you see anything?" she asked when she reached Loren, who was peeking into a rear window.

"Uh uh. There's furniture again, but it doesn't look like people live here anymore. It's like that other house we saw with papers and stuff all over the floor."

Tracie thought for a moment. "Maybe they're all together in the one house where the clothes are hanging. If it's a commune, maybe they decided to move in there."

Loren studied the house with laundry drying in the backyard. "That place's way too small for a whole bunch of people to live," she said, shaking her head. "It doesn't make much sense, but you're right. If people are living anywhere here, it's gotta be in that house."

Loren and Tracie reached the yard with the flopping clothes and stood quietly, watching the shirts and pants swaying in rhythm with the warm breeze.

"I don't know," Tracie said. "It still seems kinda quiet here. If there was a bunch of people around, we'd hear something, wouldn't we?"

Loren lowered herself to the ground, leaned against a bush, and gazed at the back of the two-story yellow shingled house. "Do you see any lights on inside?"

"No," Tracie said as she sat beside her friend. "But it's daytime and the sun is shining so that doesn't mean anything. This whole trip was your idea so what do you want to do next—peek in the window again?"

"Maybe." Loren slapped the pebbly grass with her left hand. "Damn! I thought for sure we'd just find some people who live here and talk to them outside. I don't want to tiptoe around and have that sheriff come back."

"Yeah. Well, I told you this wouldn't be as easy as you said. Maybe no one's living in this place either. Maybe they don't use any of these houses anymore."

"Then how do you explain the laundry?" Loren asked.

"Maybe they just use this house to wash their clothes."

"For a whole bunch of people? That's not enough clo..."

"Hello."

Loren stopped talking in mid-sentence at the unexpected greeting, which came from behind the bush.

The two girls turned and faced a boy, who looked like he was eleven- or twelve-years-old. His blond hair was cropped in a short crew cut and he wore a black oversized tee shirt that said "Star Trek: The Next Generation" and a pair of men's brown shorts so baggy that they would have fallen down if he hadn't been wearing a belt.

The boy stared at Loren and Tracie, but didn't speak.

"Hi," Tracie finally said, smiling. "I'm Tracie and this is my friend, Loren. What's your name?"

The boy looked puzzled and kept staring at the girls.

"It's okay," Tracie continued, speaking slowly and quietly. "You can talk to us. We won't bite you." She smiled again.

"Why would you bite me?" the boy asked, pausing between each of the five words. "People do not bite," he added in his strange staccato-like speech pattern.

"I was just trying to make a joke," Tracie explained.

"What is a 'joke'?" the boy asked.

Tracie looked at Loren, who shrugged. "Well, a joke is something that's funny—something that makes you laugh."

"Oh, a laugh, like from a smile. I can do that." The boy made a wide grin.

"That's right," Tracie said. "Very good. So we told you our names. What's your name?"

"I am called Boy 11."

"Yes," Loren said. "But what's your real name?"

The boy looked at her unhappily. "I do not understand. I am Boy 11."

Tracie grasped Loren's hand, holding it tightly. "That's fine, Boy 11. Do you live here?" She pointed to the house behind the laundry line.

"That is the school," he said.

"Oh," Tracie said. "You go to school with teachers and other children?"

Boy 11 nodded. "Teacher."

"It sounds like fun," Tracie said, smiling again.

"We do not laugh in school," the boy said, frowning at her.

Tracie waited a moment before continuing. "I'm sorry. I didn't mean to upset you, but we'd like to meet some of your family."

Boy 11 continued to frown.

"Do you have a family?" Tracie asked quietly.

Boy 11 sat across from the two girls and lowered his head. "I found books in a big box on floor one," he said in his choppy speech. "I took three books to read and I learned about 'family.' There was mother, father, sister, brother."

"Oh," Tracie said. "You don't live like the people in the book?"

The boy shook his head. "I live with Boy 4, 5, 6, 7, 8, 10 and 12."

"What about Boy 1, 2 and 3?" Tracie asked.

The boy shrugged.

"Maybe they're little," Loren suggested.

"Yeah," Tracie agreed. "But Boy 9 must be bigger. What about him?"

"I do not know," Boy 11 said in his slow clipped speech, looking sadly at Tracie. "Boy 9 is gone."

"You don't know where he went?" Loren asked.

"No." The boy looked as if he was going to cry.

Tracie quickly changed the subject. "So where do you and the other boys sleep?" she asked.

"In a house."

"Yes. But where is the house?"

"I do not know. A man takes us there after school."

"Why aren't you in school today, Boy 11?"

The boy tilted his head downward again. "I like to walk outside so I leave."

"And the teacher just lets you go?" Loren asked.

Boy 11 shrugged.

They remained quiet until Tracie continued the questioning. "Doesn't the teacher notice you aren't there?"

"I do not know," the boy said, his head still lowered.

"Wish I could've done that in school," Loren muttered.

Tracie elbowed her friend softly in the ribs. "When do you go back inside?" she asked.

"When the sun moves down," he said, raising his head and

glancing at the sky.

"Does the teacher say anything when you walk back into the room?"

Boy 11 shook his head.

"Okay, then," Tracie said. "Who else is in the school with you?"

"Boy 4, Boy 5, Boy 6, Boy..."

"All the boys you live with that you mentioned before," Loren said, interrupting him.

"Yes."

"What about girls?" Tracie asked. "Are they in your school too?"

"No."

"Where do the girls go to school?"

"I do not know," he said, shrugging.

"Wow," Loren murmured and Tracie poked her in the ribs again.

"Is there anyone else in your school?" Tracie asked.

"Woman 28."

"And what does she do?" Tracie continued.

"She makes the food, cleans the rooms, and washes the clothes." Boy 11 nodded toward the swaying laundry.

"Sounds like Cinderella," Loren muttered.

Boy 11 stood up abruptly. "I must go into the school now," he said, looking at the girls. "Do you have a story book?"

Tracie shook her head. "I'm sorry, Boy 11. We don't have any books with us. But we can come back tomorrow afternoon and bring you a book. What would you like to read about?"

"A family—a family with a mother and father and children."

"Sure." Tracie smiled. "We'll find a good book for you, Oh, and please don't tell the teacher you talked to us."

Looking confused, Boy 11 stared at Tracie. "I do not talk to Teacher."

"That's fine then," she said, smiling again. "We'll see you tomorrow, Boy 11."

"Goodbye," he said. Then he turned and ran to the house.

CHAPTER 5

"...so we're gonna stay in this part of Nevada a little longer than we'd planned," Tracie told Loren's mother late Thursday morning and then listened to Mrs. Cofton's barrage of questions. "Well, it's been more interesting here than we thought," she explained. "Lots of fun ghost towns, and you know Loren. She's been taking a ton of pictures and talking to the local people—kind of getting a feel of the place."

Tracie held the cell phone and listened to the woman's comments. "Yes," she agreed. "The people here are very friendly and we figure we'll still have time to see all the good places in California even if we spend an extra couple of days here." She listened again. "Sure. I'll call again soon—and I'll remind Loren to phone you too. Bye."

After ending the call, Tracie entered the convenience store and found Loren scowling at the wire rack of paperback books. "What's the matter?" she asked.

"I don't see anything for the kid to read," Loren complained. "These are all slutty romances or vampire and zombie stories." She shook her head and grimaced. "We can't bring this stuff to Boy 11."

"Did you ask if they have any kids' books?"

"No."

Tracie approached the tall woman behind the cash register. "Excuse me," she said. "Do you have any books for pre-teens?"

"Over there," the woman said, pointing to a small alcove.

Tracie entered the children's section and found several hardcover classic novels: *Treasure Island, Swiss Family Robinson, Little Women,* and *Peter Pan*.

As she examined the titles, Loren joined her. "Find anything?" she asked.

"I don't know," Tracie said. "None of these books is great. *Treasure Island*'s usually good for boys because it's about pirates, but there's no family. I think a family is stuck somewhere in *Swiss Family Robinson*. *Little Women*'s about a family, but it's all girls, and *Peter Pan*'s all make-believe.

"The only one I know is *Peter Pan*," Loren said. "And a kid who won't grow up in Never Neverland will only confuse Boy 11 more. From what you say, *Swiss Family Robinson* sounds the best. At least it's about a family."

"Yeah. But they're all trapped someplace."

"Maybe he'll identify with that."

"Well, we don't have much choice since there's no other store with books anywhere else around here," Tracie said. "Let's buy it and go back to the schoolhouse."

"So that's the plan for today?" Tracie asked as they drove to the hidden group of houses they had discovered the day before. "We're just gonna wait for Boy 11 to come out and then give him the book?"

"Yup, and we'll find out some more information about where he lives."

"But we already asked him that and he said he doesn't know."

"Maybe we can help him find out."

Tracie sighed. "What happened to my idea of just knocking on the door of the schoolhouse and asking the teacher?"

"The teacher may tell the sheriff about us."

"Why do you think so?"

"Boy 11 said the teacher doesn't even know when he's gone," Loren explained. "I never had a teacher like that. Did you?"

"No."

"So I'm thinking maybe the teacher's kinda like the man in the store with the water, that really weird guy."

"I guess it's possible."

"Or he could be like the sheriff—not wanting us asking questions." Loren shrugged. "Anything's possible in this place. Look at Boy 11. He doesn't have a name or a family, talks strange, and didn't even know what a joke was. Very creepy, this commune thing."

"Yeah," Tracie agreed. "Trying to find a creepy commune in the middle of nowhere is a lot more fun than being in Disneyland." She rolled her eyes at Loren and glanced at the desolate landscape.

Loren turned off the road at the same place she had found the day before. "That was easy," she explained. "I left tire marks last time." Again she parked behind the cluster of protruding rocks and the two girls walked toward the schoolhouse.

"We should've set up a meeting time," Loren said. "We don't even know when he's coming outside, just the afternoon."

"He wasn't wearing a watch," Tracie said. "And how do you know he can tell time? Remember, Boy 11's not like a regular kid."

They sat in the pebbly backyard facing the back of the building and looked at the swaying shirts and pants that were still pinned on the clothesline.

"I'm gonna read my magazine," Tracie said, opening the pages of *Us*.

"Lemme check my messages." Loren took her phone from her

jeans, stared at it, and then shook her head. "It's not working," she complained. "No signal."

"Told you we're out in Nowhereland," Tracie said. "Lucky if they even have electricity here."

"Damn." Loren crept next to her friend. "Guess I'll have to read the magazine with you."

"You can always start reading *Swiss Family Robinson,*" Tracie said. "This way you and Boy 11'll have something to talk about. No— forget that idea. I didn't like the way you questioned him yesterday. You're much too pushy. Let me do most of the talking."

"Only if you ask him the questions we decided on to get more details about where he lives."

"Let me do it slowly though. I don't want to scare..."

"Hello."

The girls looked up at the serious face of Boy 11.

"Hi," Tracie said, smiling as she quickly closed the magazine. "It's good to see you again. Did you come out because you saw us here?"

The boy nodded. He wore the same tee shirt and baggy pants as the previous day.

"Did anyone else see us?" Loren asked.

Boy 11 shrugged.

"Are you the only boy who goes outside like this?" Tracie asked.

"Sometimes Boy 12 goes with me," Boy 11 replied in his staccato-like speech.

"Here," Loren said. "We brought you something." She grinned and handed him the book.

"Swiss Fam-i-ly Rob-in-son." He paused between each syllable as he read the title out loud. "It is a book about a family." He twisted his face into a phony-looking broad smile. "I am happy."

"We're glad," Tracie said. "What are you learning in your school?"

"I learn to read and to count numbers."

"That's good," Tracie said. "What about science and social

studies?"

Boy 11 frowned. "I do not know those words."

"Huh?" Loren said. "What do you mean...?"

Before Loren could finish her question, Tracie grabbed her friend's arm and pinched it. "What else do you learn?" she asked.

"We learn how to make food, how to use a vehicle, how to use a weapon, and..."

"Sounds like very advanced boy scout stuff, more like the army," Loren muttered.

"Shh." Tracie smiled at Boy 11. "Do you learn any other things?" she continued.

"We learn our jobs," he said. "What work we will do when we leave school."

"Oh," Tracie said, still smiling. "Every boy learns a job?"

Boy 11 nodded.

"Do you choose the job?"

"What is 'choose'?" he asked as he sat across from the girls.

They remained quiet for several seconds before Tracie spoke. "To choose is to decide what you want to do," she explained. "Do you get to tell the teacher what job you'd like?"

"I do not understand," Boy 11 said. "I cannot know what job I will like."

"Yes," Tracie agreed. "But you know what things you like to do."

Boy 11 stared into the distance. "I like to look at the mountains. I would like to go there."

"Maybe you can get a job where you can travel," Loren suggested. "Like a salesman."

"What is a 'salesman'?" Boy 11 asked.

"A person who sells things to other people," Loren explained.

"What is 'sells'?"

"Okay, forget that," Tracie said. "Boy 11, what kind of jobs do you learn about in school?"

"We learn to build, to clean, to fix, and some boys learn to

34

grow food."

"Like a farmer?" Loren asked.

Boy 11 frowned at her. "I do not know what that is."

"Do you know what a camera is?" Loren asked, reaching into her jeans pocket.

The boy shook his head.

Loren twirled her smartphone. "This takes a photograph, a picture of something. Here, I'll show you." She turned toward Tracie, stared into the screen, and clicked the button. Then she quickly found the photo and showed it to Boy 11. "See?"

He stared at the small picture in awe. "How did you do that?"

"It's easy. Now I'd like to take of photo of you. Can you smile?"

The boy opened his mouth, forming another phony-looking wide grin.

Loren snapped the picture.

"Can I see it?" Boy 11 asked.

"Sure." Loren showed him the photo.

"That is me in there." He glanced at the phone. "I do not understand."

"It's just photography, something else you can learn in sch..."

"Getting back to school," Tracie interrupted. "Does the teacher train all the boys to do all of the jobs?"

He shook his head. "No. Each boy learns a job."

"What job are you learning?" Loren asked.

"I learn to build."

"That sounds like fun," Tracie said smiling. "What do you build?"

"I build a chair and a table," Boy 11 said.

"Did you get a good grade for your work?" Loren asked.

The boy looked confused again. "What is a 'grade'?"

"A good grade means the teacher liked your work," Tracie explained. "Did your chair and table come out good?"

"Yes. We sit on the chair and we use the table to eat food."

"That does sound good," Tracie said, smiling. "What else will you learn in school?"

The boy stared at her. "I will finish school at the end of the moon."

"And what happens next?" Loren asked.

Boy 11 shrugged. "I do not know."

Tracie asked her next question very quietly. "Boy 11, what happened to the other boys who already finished school? Where did they go?"

The boy sighed softly. "I do not see them," he said.

"They don't live with you anymore?" Loren asked.

He shook his head sadly.

"Are they working at their jobs?" Tracie asked.

"I do not know."

"Think hard," Tracie said. "Did you ever see any boy after he left school?"

Boy 11 closed his eyes and sat motionless. "I saw one boy," he finally said. "He was called Boy 2. He was inside the vehicle. I said his name, but he did not answer me."

"Maybe he didn't hear you," Tracie suggested.

"I was near to him as I am to you, but he did not speak."

"Do you know why he didn't talk to you?" Tracie asked.

Boy 11 glanced at his lap and spoke in a whisper. "He did not know me."

"But you lived with him and went to school with him?" Tracie continued.

"Yes."

"Then why would he forget who you were?"

Again Boy 11 spoke very quietly. "He was no longer a boy. He was one of them."

"One of them," Tracie repeated. "What do you mean by 'them'?"

"The big people."

"You mean grownups?" Loren asked.

Boy 11 nodded.

"The big people tell you what to do?" Tracie asked.

"Yes."

"What are the big people like?" Tracie continued.

"They talk to me, but they do not listen."

"What do you mean they don't listen?"

"They do not talk like you. They do not look at me."

"The man in the store," Loren whispered to Tracie. "The adults are weird like the guy in the store."

"Shh." Tracie waved her hand at her friend and smiled at the boy. "Do the big people answer your questions?"

"They say words, but they are not answers."

"And all the big people are like that?"

Boy 11 nodded sadly.

Loren inched closer to the boy and stared into his serious blue eyes. "Boy 11," she said. "Are you frightened about what will happen to you after school is finished?"

"Yes," he whispered.

Loren touched the boy's hand lightly and he flinched. "Don't be afraid," she said. "We're gonna help you."

CHAPTER 6

"So just how are we going to help him?" Tracie asked as she and Loren walked to the car after their meeting with Boy 11. "We still don't know much about him and we didn't find out anything else about where he lives." She tugged on her friend's arm. "You're not thinking about trying to take the kid back to the motel with us, are you?"

Loren shook her head. "Even if the teacher doesn't know when he's gone, someone there must count the kids. Why else would they name them all with numbers?"

"We could turn him over to the police and let them investigate," Tracie suggested. "They've done that with other cults and communes. There was that one with the Mormon guy who had all those wives and kids."

"But what if the police are the bad guys here—like that sheriff?" Loren said as they reached the car. "We can't take a chance. What did you think about that stuff he said about Boy 2?"

"Creepy. Like that guy with the water."

Loren, leaning against the car door, faced Tracie. "I have an idea about that. What if Boy 2 got a new name when he left the school? Remember, Boy 11 didn't know anything about where Boy 1, 2, and 3 are. If they're now names for little kids—or babies—then maybe the older Boy 2's now called Man 25 or Person 16—and that's why he didn't answer when Boy 11 used his old name."

"But he would've still remembered his other name," Tracie said.

"Maybe not. Boy 11 said Boy 2 had changed. Something happened to him so that he became weird, like the man in the store."

Loren sat in the driver's seat of the car and rolled down all the windows. "We're gonna follow the school bus," she told Tracie, who still stood outside.

"What!"

"Well, not really follow. I mean we're gonna listen for the bus or car—whatever comes—and then drive slowly, outta sight, behind. There's no traffic here so it shouldn't be hard to do."

"What if they notice we're there?" Tracie asked. "You just said there're no other cars so they'll be able to hear us."

"I'll be real careful, I promise."

"What if the bus comes off this road, past our car?"

"I'm gonna move the car over there so nobody'll even see us." Loren pointed to a pinyon pine tree wedged in front of the large rocks. She quickly drove the Prius behind the pine.

"See?" she said, returning to where Tracie stood watching with her arms folded. "No one'll know a car's there. C'mon." Loren pulled her friend toward the vehicle. "We gotta stand over there too, just in case."

"Lor, I don't like this at all," Tracie complained as the girl half-dragged her toward the tree.

"It'll be okay. We gotta find out where Boy 11 lives and this is the best way."

"I feel sorry for the kid too, but if these people find us, I don't think they're gonna want to be our friends. And the sheriff..."

"They're not gonna find us," Loren promised as she positioned Tracie and herself between the car and the bush. "Now take out the magazine and we'll read while we wait and listen."

About twenty minutes later, Loren tapped her friend on the shoulder. "Do you hear it?" she whispered.

Tracie nodded, recognizing the sound of a vehicle's engine near the cluster of houses.

"C'mon," Loren said as she darted into the car and quickly fastened her seat belt. As soon as Tracie settled into the passenger seat, Loren began inching the Prius toward the nearby group of houses.

"You're making too much noise," Tracie complained.

"I can't help it that I'm driving over pebbles. But the car or bus didn't come through here so we're already way behind. It must've come down that little dirt road. I'm gonna go very slow and keep listening for the other car. There're no street signs, but you keep track of where we're going—when we turn and any landmarks you see."

Tracie nodded and took a pad and pencil from the glove compartment.

The late afternoon was eerily quiet except for the sound of the other vehicle in the distance. The girls didn't speak as Loren drove about ten miles an hour, passing the schoolhouse and the vacant houses, and then guiding the Prius onto the dirt road. She continued driving along the smoother surface, following the steady engine noise.

After several miles, the sound abruptly stopped. Loren immediately hit the brakes and swung off the road, parking behind a large sagebrush. "We're walking from here," she whispered as she crept out of the car and carefully closed the door. "I don't see the house, but it can't be very far."

"We're out in the open here," Tracie murmured, joining Loren and staring at the bare landscape. "What if someone sees us?"

"Nobody's looking. And we're gonna be real quiet." Loren glanced at the scrubby grass. "At least the ground's not all rocks. Let's go."

The girls walked without speaking alongside the dirt road, not seeing anything but a few shrubs and scattered large rocks. The terrain was mostly flat until they reached a small hill. When they climbed over the incline, they saw a solitary two-story brown-shingled house about a hundred yards below. A black van was parked in front of the building.

"Now what?" Tracie whispered as the girls lowered themselves to the ground to avoid being seen.

"Now we watch."

"Watch for what?"

"Well, maybe whoever drove the van will come out and drive it away."

"If the driver goes back the way he came, he'll see us."

Loren paused. "You're right," she finally said. "There's really no place to hide up here."

"So maybe we should go now?" Tracie suggested. "We don't want to get stuck here in the dark. We didn't even bring a flashlight."

"Damn," Loren muttered. "I should've thought of that."

"No, you shouldn't have. We don't want to be poking around here in the dark, even with flashlights. Listen, now that we know where the boys live—and it's an easy drive—we can check the place out during the day when there's less chance someone'll be here. Think about it, Lor. My idea makes more sense."

"I guess," Loren whispered. "If we head back here tomorrow morning around ten, the boys should be in school."

Friday morning, Loren swung the Prius onto the pebbly ground by the rock formation and continued the bumpy ride toward the dirt road.

"I don't like driving past the school," Tracie said. "It's so quiet here and the car's the only noise. Someone inside there can hear us or see us."

"I'm thinking the teacher doesn't know or doesn't care—like Boy 11 told us," Loren explained. "Besides, we can't walk that far in the hot sun, out in the open. If we run into the sheriff, or someone else, we'd have no way to escape so we gotta take the chance and drive."

Tracie picked up her cell phone and stared at it. "Still no signal here," she said. "Another reason to be real careful 'cause we can't even call for help."

Loren smiled. "That's why we are being real careful." She reached the area in front of the hill and turned off the road, parking behind the largest group of rocks.

"You can still see the car," Tracie complained.

"I know, but there's nothing around here that hides it. I figure no one's gonna come and we shouldn't take too long scouting this place out. Let's go take a look at how Boy 11 and the other boys live when they're 'home.'"

"I wonder where the girls live," Tracie whispered as they scampered down the small hill.

"Yeah, me too—but right now, let's go see the boys' home."

At the bottom of the hill, the brown house stood alone and silent; the black van was gone. Loren held her finger over her lips as she and Tracie dashed toward their destination. The two girls scooted to the back of the house, crouching as they darted, until they reached a picture window and a sliding glass door, both covered by vertical blinds.

"Damn, I was hoping to look inside," Loren whispered. "Lemme check if there's a window here that we can see into." She crept to the right side of the building and lifted her head high enough to examine and pull on the window. "This one's locked and it's got a shade down," she murmured to Tracie, who trailed behind.

The girls tested all the windows along the sides of the house and each one was locked and covered. Loren quickly tried the front door too, but it wouldn't budge.

"Let's just forget about this idea," Tracie said.

"No." Loren sat with her arms around her knees on the rocky ground in the back of the house and shook her head. "We have to get inside somehow."

"You're gonna break into the house?" Tracie whispered. "Then the sheriff can arrest us for real."

Loren gazed at the sliding glass door. "These things are pretty easy to open," she muttered, standing up and pulling at the handle. "If there's no stick holding it, I think can bust this lock."

"That's breaking in!"

"Shh." Loren grabbed her key chain, found the little penknife attachment on it, and jiggled the lock with the blade until she heard a slight click. "We're in," she said, smiling at her friend.

Tracie followed Loren into the house and closed the back door softly. The air smelled stale and, although it was only mid-morning, the indoor temperature was already verging on hot. "We shouldn't be doing this," Tracie said.

"Shh. Don't say anything until we're sure no one's home."

The girls stood inside the family room, except it wasn't being used as a playroom or recreation space. Instead, the room was a storage area, with cans of food and numerous cardboard boxes piled on the floor.

When Loren and Tracie tiptoed into the adjacent kitchen, they found walls covered in a pale yellow geometric wallpaper, which was peeling in several places. Otherwise, the room was an ordinary kitchen, featuring the basic appliances. It was clean and bare, with no objects cluttering the counters.

Loren opened the door of the pantry and peered inside. Jars of peanut butter and jelly, cans of tuna, and boxes of cereal filled the shelves. Shrugging, she reached for the refrigerator handle and pulled it open. Three milk containers and an unmarked bottle of water filled the top shelf. She tapped Tracie on the shoulder and pointed to the water.

Tracie nodded.

Next, the two girls peeked into the dining room, which held a large unvarnished wooden table and ten chairs, each of them different. The room had no decorations.

A living room on the ground floor contained an old 21-inch television, two ripped leather couches, and a wooden cocktail table riddled with scratches. A stained beige carpet covered the floor.

"It's not pretty, but at least there's a TV here," Tracie whispered.

"Look at this," Loren said, leaning on one of the sofas and tapping the fingerprint-smudged white wall behind it. "See the nail marks here? There used to be pictures hung up. Wonder why they took them all down."

"This place doesn't look like a home where kids live," Tracie said softly. "There're no toys or anything."

"Maybe there's more stuff for them upstairs," Loren said. "That's probably where the boys sleep. We should be okay going up 'cause I'm sure no one's here now."

The girls climbed the worn green-carpeted staircase to the second floor and faced three rooms. Entering the first room on the left, they found four mattresses shoved together in the middle of the floor, nearly touching. Every mattress contained a pillow and was neatly covered with a white sheet. Along each of the walls—papered in a clowns-holding-balloons pattern—stood a five-drawer plastic cart on wheels with the number "4," "5," "6," or "7" written on the front in magic marker.

Loren squeezed her body to one side of the room, opened the top drawer of the "4" cart, and looked inside. "It's got socks and underwear here," she said, pulling out a small white shirt and reading the label. "Size 6."

"That's for a kid," Tracie said.

"Yeah, Boy 4, I'd bet." Loren put the undershirt back into the drawer. "Stuff is piled in very neat," she said. "Doesn't look like the way a little boy would handle his clothes. Lemme check the other ones." Quickly, she rushed to the other carts and opened a drawer of each. "They're all like that—full of clothes folded real neat."

"Well, we've talked to Boy 11 and he's not your typical kid," Tracie pointed out.

Loren shuddered. "If this is the way kids live in a commune, I don't like it. C'mon. Let's check out the other rooms. Boy 11 must sleep next door."

The girls walked into the middle room, another bedroom identical to the first, with four mattresses and four carts on wheels. Besides the dirty pink walls, the only difference was the carts were numbered "8," "10," "11," and "12."

Loren sidled to the wall with the "11" cart and peered inside. "Just like the other ones, only this is a size 12," she said, lifting an undershirt.

"Yeah, even though it's painted pink, this has gotta be the older boys' room," Tracie said. "But why wouldn't they at least paint it blue? And I don't like the missing number 9."

"Me neither. Let's look at what else is up here." After darting into the hallway, Loren ran inside the third room. "This is nothing," she said when Tracie entered.

It was another storage area, with quilts, blankets, and pillows piled on one side and textbooks, pens, pencils, paper and other school-related supplies on the opposite side.

"Where are the toys and games?" Tracie asked.

"Not here. Maybe these kids don't have any fun." Loren knelt on the floor and picked up one of the textbooks. "These look old," she said, opening it. "This one's a math book for little kids. There's an Elko County Schools label in the front with kids' names written in. The last name listed is Stacy Covington in September, 1990."

"That's a long time ago."

"Yeah, and Boy 11 didn't even know what science and social studies are." Loren ran her finger along the spines of the other books. "These are all math and reading, no other subjects."

"Maybe these are just the school books they don't use anymore."

"Ya think?" Loren shrugged. "Don't these commune people have to give their kids a real education, not just teach them how to fight and build things? Somebody should be checking."

Tracie leaned against the door and shook her head. "Doesn't look like anyone is." She glanced at her watch. "Lor, we've been in this house for a half hour already and I don't think there's much else to see. Let's get outta here before someone comes back."

"Yeah, I guess." Loren stood up and they left the room, peeking quickly into the nondescript bathroom before climbing down the stairs and returning to the family room. Then the girls opened the sliding glass door, stepped outside, and shut the door.

"I hope they don't realize the lock is broken," Tracie said.

"I've got a gut feeling that these people don't notice much of anything," Loren said as they both dashed away from the house toward the car.

CHAPTER 7

Sheriff Tom Dugan twirled his cowboy hat in his chubby fingers Friday afternoon as he stood patiently in the lavishly furnished office waiting to be acknowledged. Despite the outside heat, the room was cool, almost too chilly. Finally, the grossly fat young woman sitting in a palatial chair behind an enormous rosewood desk looked up at him and smiled.

"We may have a little problem, Merlynn," he began.

"What do you mean by 'little problem'?" the woman asked.

"I saw some fresh tire marks on the old road near the boys' school this morning. Wasn't nothin' there a week ago."

"But that's not even a road anymore," Merlynn said, stuffing a chocolate cupcake into her mouth. "What would someone be doing driving over there?"

"I don't know."

"Did you see anyone suspicious lately around Corsonia?" she asked as she finished eating the cream-filled cupcake, wiped her mouth with a napkin, and grabbed another from the Hostess box on her desk.

"Just a couple of teenage girls snoopin' around the old shopping center a few days ago. But I'm sure I scared them off."

"Well, maybe you didn't. I'm paying you a lot of money to make sure we don't get any curious strangers poking their heads into my business." The woman stopped licking the squiggles off the icing and scowled at the sheriff. "You understand, Tom?" She nodded her head, causing her hefty jowls to bob up and down.

"Yes, Merlynn. I understand."

"Good." She smiled at the man as she continued to munch on the cupcake. "Check it out and report back to me tomorrow."

"I will," the sheriff said. Then, after a quick bow, he turned and left the office.

Merlynn finished eating the cupcake, pushed the chair away, leaned on the desk for support, and stood. After waddling to the window, she stared at the sheriff as he stepped into his car and drove down the steep hill.

"He better find out what's going on," she muttered. "I don't ask him to do much to earn his salary." She snorted, remembering how she had recruited Dugan for her project thirteen years ago. It had been so easy. But then, what else would you expect from a corrupt politician?

He had been the mayor of Corsonia and was about to be indicted for embezzling town funds. She had already devised her plan, needed an eager assistant, and he was the perfect choice. His wife had recently left him so he was all alone. She paid the money he owed and Dugan was hers. Now he was the sheriff and, for election purposes, the town's current mayor was someone named "John Smith." *Not that anyone really voted.* She chuckled at the thought of the people in Corsonia casting votes. *What a hoot!*

And Dugan hardly had to do any policing other than driving around the town and making sure no strangers started asking probing questions. The locals had been fine since the beginning and even helped by spreading the story about the commune, telling everyone that the people in Corsonia were weird, lived by themselves, and didn't want any contact with outsiders. The couple of times the neighboring townspeople had tasted the bottled water—and conked out—kept them even further away.

It was a perfect scheme as long as no one investigated too closely. *But after all this time, who would care?* The relatives had given up long ago, assuming their Corsonian brethren wanted nothing to do with them anymore. *That's true,* Merlynn thought. Her people really didn't care about their friends and relatives. In fact, they didn't care about anything.

She chuckled as she returned to the desk and picked up another cupcake.

Loren turned the car off the road at the spot with the tire tracks and once again hid the Prius behind the rocks. Then she and Tracie walked to the backyard of the school building, where assorted items of clothing still flapped in the wind, and waited.

"I know we told Boy 11 we'd be here today, but that's before we realized it was Saturday," Tracie said. "Are you sure he has school today?"

Loren shrugged and opened a magazine. "I don't know. He didn't say he wouldn't be here."

"Since we can't pick a time to meet, we could be waiting all afternoon for nothing."

"Yeah," Loren agreed, glancing up. "But we need to ask him more questions about the grownups to find out what they do and where they live."

"I'm sure Boy 11 doesn't know any of that," Tracie said. "He couldn't even tell us where he lives and there's no one else here we can ask."

"Those adults are so weird, they probably wouldn't even care if we followed..."

"No!" Tracie interrupted. "You can't be sure of that. We've only met two of them—one was real strange and the other was real mean. You don't know for sure that they're all gonna be like the man in the store. Maybe there's more like the sheriff."

"From what Boy 11 told us, the grownups are all like the man in the store. His teacher doesn't even seem to know if he leaves the classroom—remember? So maybe we should check out the teacher—wait to see who picks him up today and then tail him to where he lives."

"What if it's the sheriff who drives him home?"

"I never thought about that," Loren admitted. "But we need to do something."

Tracie checked her watch. "It's already 3:30, and all the other times, Boy 11's been here by now. We can't even tell if anyone's in the building. It's always so quiet."

"Maybe he's got a test or something today."

"You think they have tests in this school? He didn't even know what grades were."

"Well, let's stick around for another few minutes, just in..."

"Hello."

The girls stopped talking and looked up at the serious face of Boy 11.

"How do you always do that, sneak up on us like that?" Loren asked.

"What is 'sneak up'?" Boy 11 asked in his strange staccato speech. He wore a plain navy tee shirt that was so big, it nearly covered his baggy brown shorts.

"It means you move so quietly that we can't hear you," Loren explained.

"I must move quietly. I am not allowed to make noise."

"You can never be loud?" Tracie asked.

"No."

"Even the babies?" Loren asked.

"They cry when they are very small. Then they learn to be quiet."

"Oh," Tracie murmured, not knowing what else to say.

"We weren't sure you'd be in school today 'cause it's Saturday," Loren said, changing the subject.

"I am in school every day."

"Don't you have time off to play and have fun?" she continued.

Boy 11 shook his head. "We do not have a time for when we play and have fun."

"Do you have any toys—things you play with?" Tracie asked.

"No."

"What about playing ball?" Loren asked.

Boy 11 looked puzzled.

"You throw a ball from one person to another, like this," she explained, picking up a stick and tossing it to Tracie, who caught the branch with both hands. "Works better with something round, like a ball."

Boy 11 nodded. "Yes. We do that. We throw sticks and rocks. Sometimes we throw pillows at each other in the room where we sleep."

"Oh, a game," Loren said.

"Yes. We do not make noise. But we like to throw pillows."

"Who is in the house with all the boys?" Tracie asked.

"Man 36 stays with us."

Tracie continued the questioning. "Only one man?"

"Yes."

"What does Man 36 do in the house?"

"He makes the food and gives us clothes to wear."

"When you eat, what do you drink?"

"We drink water. Sometimes we have milk."

Tracie glanced quickly at Loren. "The water you drink, is it in a bottle?"

Boy 11 shook his head. "We cannot drink the bottles of water. The water for us comes out from the sink."

"So only the grownups—the big people—drink the bottles of water?" Loren asked.

Boy 11 nodded. "It is forbidden."

"For the boys?" Tracie asked.

"Yes."

Loren moved closer to Boy 11. "Did any of the boys ever drink the water from a bottle?" she asked softly.

"Boy 9 did."

"What happened to him?" Loren continued.

"He went to sleep."

"And then?"

Boy 11 studied his dirty white sneakers and sighed before he spoke. "Boy 9 took a bottle of water to the room. He was asleep when we went to school." Then, raising his head, Boy 11 gazed sadly at the girls. "We came back from school and he was gone."

They were all quiet for nearly a minute until Tracie spoke. "What does Man 36 do when you're at school all day?"

Boy 11 shrugged. "I do not know."

"But he doesn't stay in the house?"

The boy shook his head. "The big people go to work." He looked at the ground and frowned. "I will go to work soon too."

"Don't worry," Loren said. "We'll help..."

Tracie grabbed the girl's arm to shut her up. "Do the big people drive to work?" she continued. "In cars?"

"A yellow bus comes to the house. Man 36 goes in there." The boy looked up. "I have seen him go into the bus when I go to school."

"Other grownups are in that bus?" Tracie asked.

"Yes. I have seen their faces in the windows."

"Thank you," Tracie said, smiling. "That's very important information."

Boy 11 stared at her, a confused expression on his face.

"It'll be okay," Loren said, reaching out to touch the boy's arm.

He flinched and jumped back.

Loren quickly withdrew her hand. "Sorry. I didn't mean to upset you."

"I must go now."

"Why'd you make me stop talking?" Loren asked as Boy 11 dashed toward the schoolhouse.

"I wanted to find out what he knows about the grownup living at his home and I didn't want to get off the subject and start talking about what's gonna happen to him when he has to go to work." Tracie shook her head. "We don't even know if we can help him, Lor."

"Yes. We can."

"Really? And just how are we gonna do that?"

"We follow the yellow bus."

"What?" Tracie jumped up and stared at her friend. "You are out of your mind!"

"Shh. Sit down and listen to me." With a tug on Tracie's arm, Loren eased her friend into a sitting position. "We don't know where the adults live and we have no easy way of finding that out. But, if we follow the bus, we do have a way of finding out where a whole bunch of them work."

"How will that help us with Boy 11?"

"I'm not sure, but I have a gut feeling that it will."

Tracie sat quietly, processing Loren's idea. "What if they see us following them?" she finally asked.

"I'll stay far back, but I don't think these weirdos would notice us or even care if they saw us."

"You do realize that we have no idea what time they go to work?"

"I'm guessing it's very early," Loren said. "We should be here by six o'clock tomorrow. And you know what makes even more sense? We should follow the bus after they leave work. That way we'd know where they live."

"Let me get this straight: You want us to be here at the crack of dawn and follow the bus to wherever it goes and then spend the whole day out here and then follow the bus back to where it takes these people?"

"Yeah."

"What about the sheriff?"

Loren shrugged. "If we want to help Boy 11, we have to take a chance that he's not looking for us. Besides, we haven't done anything wrong."

Tracie sighed. "I don't have a better idea so I guess we should go to bed real early tonight. Then we've gotta pack a ton of food—and lots and lots of water."

CHAPTER 8

Sheriff Dugan pulled his black Ford Explorer off CR-766 early Saturday evening and stepped outside to examine the tire tracks on the pebbly ground. "No way of knowin' if these are the same marks I saw yesterday or fresh ones," he muttered. Taking off his tan cowboy hat, he wiped his sweaty brow with the palm of his hand. *What'm I gonna tell Merlynn?*

The sheriff put his hat back on his head and leaned against the SUV, considering his options. If he came back here every day to check, he'd never be sure if the marks were new. "Guess I could take pictures," he mumbled. *Nah.* He shook his head, realizing it would be difficult to distinguish the tracks in a photo.

"Damn!" he said. "Gotta do a stakeout." Then he smiled softly, liking the word "stakeout," which he associated with real police work. *Okay. Hide out in the rocks tomorrow. See if anyone comes here.*

Feeling pleased with himself, he got into the car and headed to Merlynn's house.

A little before six o'clock on Sunday morning, the day already coated in bright sunlight, Loren drove to the usual spot. After turning off the road, she steered the car through the pebbles, past the school building, and onto the small road leading to the boys' quarters. Once again, she parked the Prius behind the largest pile of rocks and she and Tracie walked quickly to the edge of the hill overlooking the brown house. Then, finding an area of dense scrubby grass, the girls stretched out on the ground and stared at the building below.

"No bus or van there," Tracie said, pointing to the driveway. "What if they just go to church today?"

"You really think these weirdos are religious? Besides, Boy 11 said he goes to school every day. We're fine. Don't worry."

"It's awfully quiet and I don't see any lights. Maybe we're here too late."

"These people are always quiet so that doesn't mean anything." Loren squinted, trying to get a clearer look at the windows. "The shades are all closed like before so we don't know if the lights are on or not. Hey—maybe they don't have electricity."

"They do too, dummy! You opened the refrigerator—the bottle of bad water, remember? And we saw a dishwasher and lamps and even a TV."

"Don't call me names, you wuss." Loren stuck out her tongue. "I just forgot. Anyway, if it wasn't for me, you wouldn't be doing this—you wanted to go to California." She took her phone from her pants pocket and turned it on. "Still no signal so maybe they do have electricity, but they don't have phones out here."

"Maybe not cell phones, but everyone has some kinda phone."

"These cult people are not like everyone," Loren said as she turned off the phone and tucked it back into her jeans. "That water..."

"Yeah, the water," Tracie agreed. "You drank it and fell asleep, but now you're fine. How come?"

Loren shrugged. "I'm not sure. There's gotta be more to it than just drinking the water one time. Maybe you have to keep drinking it to turn into a weirdo."

"I guess. You know, Lor, we should've told someone back home what we're really doing here, instead of just saying we're checking out more ghost towns and taking pictures."

"Then they would've made us stop."

"But what if something happens to us?"

"Nothing's gonna happen to us, Trace."

"At least they could find our bodies."

"Shut up! We told our parents the name of the motel."

"Lotta good that'll do if those crazy people kill us way out here."

"Yeah, but I promise we're gonna be okay."

"Thank you, oh wise one," Tracie said, bowing her head in mock reverence.

Loren slapped her friend's arm playfully and then held on. "Listen..."

The distinct rumbling of a vehicle's engine resounded in the distance.

"Will they see us?" Tracie whispered.

"I don't know. Let's scrunch down real low and hope it's one of the weird people driving and I'm right that they don't care at all about us."

As the girls watched, a black van passed by quickly on the nearby road and continued toward the house below.

"That's for the boys," Loren said.

Tracie nodded.

"Now let's see what happens to the man here after the boys go to school."

Less than five minutes later, the girls heard the sound of another approaching vehicle. From their positions—face down on the ground—they saw a yellow school bus zoom past them.

"It's full of people inside," Loren whispered.

Tracie pointed to the boys' house below as a bearded ponytailed man, carrying a black lunch pail, walked out the front door, and locked it. Then he stepped into the bus, which immediately turned around and backtracked onto the small dirt road.

"C'mon," Loren said and dashed to the car with Tracie. After turning on the ignition, Loren waited until the bus was nearly out of sight.

"Here we go." Loren put the Prius into gear and followed the bus, keeping far behind. "It's so quiet here that we can just listen," she said, rolling down her window. "Try to remember how we're going."

Tracie nodded and again took the small notebook and pen from the glove compartment.

The bus continued on the road for about a half a mile and then turned right onto an even smaller dirt road. After several miles along bumpy terrain, the bus made a left turn onto worn-down brush and climbed a wooded hill.

"This isn't even a road," Tracie whispered as she jotted down the bus' route. "Can this car handle it?"

"If the bus goes up here, we can too."

When she no longer heard the sound of the other engine, Loren immediately looked for a place to pull off the makeshift road.

"Here," Tracie said, indicating a narrow opening in the brush. Loren turned the Prius toward the right and drove it a few yards out of the pathway.

The girls stepped quietly out of the car and Loren looked at the hill in front of them. "We gotta go up there and check it out," she said.

Tracie shook her head. "I don't know about this plan. If anyone comes up here, they'll see the car. There's no good place to hide it."

Loren glanced at a nearby clump of silvery-white sagebrush and pointed. "How about if I drive behind there? It's kinda the same color."

"I guess."

After Loren moved the car, the girls stared at the camouflage attempt.

Tracie shrugged. "That didn't work. You can still see the car."

"Yeah, but you don't notice it that much. Let's go see what those cult people are doing. I'm real curious. I mean, what could be all the way up here?"

The girls, each wearing a backpack filled with food and four bottles of water, climbed until they reached a sturdy chain-link fence that encircled the small mountain. Two bands of razor wire covered the top of the enclosure and the entrance gate in front of them was securely chained.

"I guess they don't want any company," Tracie said, pointing to two signs posted on the fence. The first read "**Private Property**" and the second warned "**No Trespassing!**" She turned toward Loren. "What now, oh great leader?"

"Well, we can't climb over this so let's scoot around and see if we can find an opening underneath that we can squeeze through."

Stepping through brush and small trees, the two girls strode along the fence, passing more of the posted warning signs as they checked for a way to get inside.

"I don't know, Lor," Tracie said, shaking the heavy metal barrier without feeling any movement. "This fence's pretty new and strong. It's not even rusty."

"Yeah, but an animal still could've done something to it on the bottom, digging it up somewhere." Loren continued walking with her head down, studying the ground next to the fence.

Halfway around the perimeter, Loren squatted on the dusty earth and pulled on the chains. "See, I was right," she said. "Come here and help me push this loose part up some more."

Tracie dropped to her knees and tugged on the bottom of the fence, which was no longer securely attached to the ground. The girls managed to stretch and raise the metal links enough to create a narrow opening.

"We can't fit through there," Tracie said.

"Lift up the fence as high as you can and just watch me." After handing Tracie her backpack, Loren stretched flat onto the ground, scrunched head down, and wriggled through the hole. "See? No sweat." She sat up, spread out her hands, and smiled.

Tracie shoved both backpacks through the opening, looked at her friend through the metal links, and sighed. "I guess if you could get through, I can too. I'm shorter and skinnier. Okay, here goes." Following an unsuccessful first attempt, she managed to squeeze her body to the other side of the fence.

"So here we are," Tracie said, wiping the dirt off her tee shirt and jeans. "What now?"

Loren pushed the fence back in place. Then she tore a piece of brown paper wrapping from her sandwich and stuck it near the opening. "I'm gonna use this as a marker," she explained. "Now let's head back to the entrance and see what's going on up here."

Walking close to the fence, the girls returned to the chained front gate. Loren signaled Tracie to move forward along the edge of the interior road and they continued silently until they spotted the yellow school bus.

"Look," Tracie whispered. "Two more." She pointed to a trio of empty buses, next to a gray SUV, in a small parking lot. "But where are all the people?"

Without answering the question, Loren marched past the buses, climbed to the top of the hill, and studied the scene below.

"What is all that?" Tracie asked as she reached her friend.

The bowl-shaped valley contained a tall triangular ladder-like wooden structure, several silos, and a few small stone buildings wedged into the surrounding hill. The interior landscape contained few bushes, very little grass—and no people.

"So?" Tracie asked again. "What's going on down there?"

Loren sat on the ground, still looking at the valley below. "From the old photos I've seen, I'm pretty sure this is some kind of a mine." She turned to face Tracie. "The reason we don't see any people is because they're probably all underground, working in the mine."

Tracie sat next to Loren and crossed her legs. "But that doesn't seem like the kind of job people in a cult would do. Boy 11 talked about being a carpenter and said other kids were studying fixing or cleaning and stuff like that. He didn't say anything about learning to be a miner."

Loren thought for a second. "Maybe you don't have to learn stuff at school to do this. Maybe it's just a lot of hard work, you know, swinging an axe and hammering."

"What do you think they're mining for?"

"Well, all those mines in the ghost towns around here were for silver or gold."

"But the towns died because the silver or gold ran out."

"Yeah," Loren said, nodding at Tracie. "But people are working in this mine—three busloads full."

At eight o'clock Sunday morning, Sheriff Dugan drove off the county road onto the pebbly ground where he had seen the freshly-made tire tracks and parked his black SUV behind the largest rock formation. Then he stepped out to make sure he was hidden from both the asphalt road and the former road that led to the nearby houses.

"I'm good," he muttered as he removed a lawn chair and set it near the car. Next he reached into the front seat and scooped up a thermos and a mystery novel he had been meaning to read. Finally, he sat in the lawn chair, picked up the book, and took a sip of coffee. "Ah," he murmured. *Pretend it's a picnic or day at the beach.*

He unbuttoned the top of his golf shirt and lifted his brown Stetson to wipe a bead of sweat from his forehead. *More like a beach day without the beach. Early in the morning and already so goddamn hot.*

But he had told Merlynn he'd be doing the stakeout today and she was expecting his report. After uttering a sigh, he gazed at the book in his hand and opened it.

Still sitting at the top of the hill, Tracie glanced at the imposing perimeter fence and shook her head. "I'm getting creeped out in this place. I feel like a rat trapped in a big cage. What if they have a guard and he finds us?"

"We've already been here for a half hour and we only saw one person walking around the bottom—not up here—so calm down," Loren said as she snapped another photo. "Anyway, no one's looking for us."

"Okay. Then what do you want to do—spend the rest of the day sitting out here in this heat, taking pictures and staring at nothing?" Tracie pulled a bottle of water out of her backpack and took a sip.

Loren shoved the smartphone in her jeans pocket and poked at the pebbly ground with her fingers. "Yeah. You're right. We can't do anything from up where we are."

"You're not thinking that we should go down to the mine?" Tracie stared at her friend wide-eyed.

"No. We can't do that. It's much too dangerous, but..."

"What do you mean 'but'?"

"I want to find out more about what's happening down there. I've got an idea, but I need to understand the mine setup more clearly."

"Loren, we are not going down there!"

"We don't have to, not now anyway. C'mon. Let's make our way back to the opening in the fence and see if we can get to the schoolhouse from here. I want to ask Boy 11 a couple more questions."

By the time Loren and Tracie found the dirt road to the boys' school, it was already late Sunday morning.

"I thought you were making notes about the roads we're taking," Loren complained.

"I am, but these aren't real roads. There are no street signs or anything to go by out here. What should I've written: 'Make a left turn at the second bush'?"

"Then how're we gonna get back to the mine?"

"That's why I asked you for the number of miles every time we turned."

"Yeah, but we made a couple of wrong turns."

"Still, it's the best way I can think of to go back there unless you want to follow the bus again."

Tracie and Loren rode quietly until they reached the schoolhouse, still easily identified by the laundry line of drying clothing. After Loren parked the car in the driveway of one of the nearby abandoned homes, the girls walked toward the gently swaying tee shirts and shorts.

"We've never been here in the morning," Tracie said. "How will Boy 11 even know to look for us?"

Loren pointed to the windows in the rear of the house, all of them halfway opened. "I'm hoping maybe he's watching," she said.

After lowering herself to the ground, Tracie reached into her backpack for another bottle of water. "Man, it's hot," she said, taking a drink. "I hope we don't have to sit out here till the middle of the afternoon."

Loren lay face up on the ground and closed her eyes. "Yeah, I know what you mean. But I've gotta talk to Boy 11."

Hearing the sound of voices nearby, Loren rubbed her eyes and stretched. "Did I fall asleep?" she asked.

"Yup," Tracie said. "Say hello to our visitors."

Loren blinked and saw two boys sitting opposite and staring at her. One was Boy 11, dressed in a blue tee shirt and the same baggy brown shorts. The other boy, tall and lanky with cropped black hair, wore jeans and a skintight dirty white shirt with the words, "Beavis and Butt-head" and the faces of two smirking cartoon teens pictured underneath.

"Hi," Loren said, grinning at the serious-looking boys. "Boy 11, who's your friend?"

"This is Boy 12. I told him I talked to you."

"It's nice to meet you, Boy 12."

The dark-haired boy continued to stare at Loren, but didn't smile or say anything.

"He does not see many girls," Boy 11 explained.

"Nor do you," Boy 12 said, his voice much deeper than Boy 11's, but with the same choppy cadence.

"I see pictures of girls in books."

"It is differ..."

"Okay, boys," Tracie interrupted. "We're trying to help you. Boy 12, are you also leaving school to go to work soon?"

Boy 12 nodded seriously. "After the full moon."

"And you are afraid about what will happen?" Tracie continued.

"Yes." He lowered his head.

"To help you, we need to know more about the water in the bottles that only the big people drink," Loren said. "How many times a day do they drink a bottle of water?"

The boys looked at each other, blank expressions on both their faces. "We do not know," Boy 11 said with a shrug. "We do not see many big people."

"What about when the teacher—or Man 36 or Woman 28—is with you?" Loren asked.

"Man 36 drinks a bottle of water at the evening meal," Boy 11 said.

"And at breakfast?" Loren probed.

"I do not see him drink the water then," Boy 11 said.

"He drinks milk with us at the morning meal," Boy 12 offered, nodding his head.

"How does he get the bottles of water?" Tracie asked. "Is it from a truck?"

"Yes. A vehicle brings the bottles to the door," Boy 11 said.

"How often?" Tracie asked. "Does it come each day?"

Boy 11 nodded. "We see the bottles at the house."

"When we return from school," Boy 12 added.

"Does Man 36 take water with his lunch when he gets on the bus to go to work?" Loren asked.

The boys looked at each other again. Then Boy 11 turned to Loren and shrugged. "We do not know."

"When's the next full moon again?" Loren asked after the boys had returned to school and she drove toward CR-766. "I remember you said it was soon."

"The full moon's on Friday night."

"That doesn't give us much time to figure out a way to help Boy 11 and Boy 12 and anyone else who's 'graduating' from this school."

"No. Especially since we don't even know where the grownups live."

"That may not matter. We already know where most of them work."

"How will that help us?" Tracie frowned at her friend. "Please tell me you're not thinking about going down into that mine."

"No. We don't have to do that. But it's all about the water so I think I have an idea about what we can do."

As Loren drove past the rock formations and continued onto the county road toward the motel, she outlined her plan while Tracie listened attentively. Neither girl noticed the black SUV wedged in the hiding place where they usually parked.

CHAPTER 9

Late Sunday afternoon, Sheriff Dugan stood, hat in hand, in Merlynn's palatial office waiting for a signal to speak. Finally, the obese woman looked up from the magazine she was reading and smiled sweetly at him. "Yes, Tom," she said. "You have some new information?"

"It's those same two girls who must've made the tire tracks. I hid behind the rocks and, this afternoon, I saw them drive that silver car onto the main road from the old path near the boys' school."

"But you never saw them go in there?" She grabbed a cupcake from the Hostess box on her desk and carefully removed the cellophane wrapping.

"No."

"You told me you were going to hide in the rocks in the morning."

"I was there real early so they must've gone off the road at another place."

"Interesting," she murmured, taking a bite of the cake. "What could they be doing here?"

"Causing trouble, that's for sure. And it was after I told them to get lost."

"Not to worry," Merlynn said, finishing her cupcake. "I'll get our people on it this evening. Be here at quarter to eight." She wiped a dab of cream from her lip and licked her fat finger. "The problem is about to be solved."

After the sheriff left, Merlynn gobbled another cupcake and considered the situation. Her life was perfect right now. She had all the time she needed for the two things she loved doing most: experimenting and eating.

"Thirteen years of bliss," she muttered, leaning back in her chair.

Merlynn was a scientific genius. At a very early age, she had experimented with her first chemistry set, creating extraordinary potions that were acclaimed by local scientists. Her parents had encouraged her efforts and were thrilled with her success.

As a preteen, Merlynn became fascinated with research on mind-control and read voraciously about early CIA experiments, the documentation readily available on the Internet through the Freedom of Information Act. She began putting all her efforts into developing a mind-control formula, never confiding in anyone—not even her parents—about her change of direction. To hide her true objective, she ordered a wide variety of drugs and, when someone asked what she was working on, she always said, "A cure for cancer." The person would smile, walk away, and leave her alone.

Even then, Merlynn knew people wouldn't approve of her work, but she never cared. She delved into the chemical labyrinth—an engrossing riddle, even for a genius, since there were about seven hundred mind-altering drugs and each produced a different effect. Finding the right combination—that was the challenge.

Because her formula wouldn't work with animals, she needed human subjects and Merlynn tried her first concoctions on kids she knew. The dose was always tasteless and added surreptitiously to a liquid. She had some early failures: One girl in her class died of a heart attack; a boy in her neighborhood became paranoid—he kept seeing grasshoppers and had to swat them away from his face.

But there were also successes. Merlynn ordered a twelve-year-old boy to steal fifty dollars from his mother's wallet and give the money to her. Then she had him forget the experience. He did exactly as he was told. Using the same formula, she instructed a nine-year-old girl to jump off a tall tree. The girl jumped, broke her leg, and was never able to explain why she had leapt.

Merlynn used the successful formula as a base, but it still wasn't potent enough for her needs. She wanted total control. Then she read about a Haitian voodoo cult in which a plant—a "zombi cucumber"—acted like a powerful psychotic drug, producing amnesia so the subject could be convinced that he or she was dead. Although the brain didn't die, the victim's mind stopped working, enabling the person to be "reborn" by the programmer as a zombie slave.

"Zombie slave," she had murmured, smiling at the appealing image. "That would work." She added several herbs to her formula and continued to make adjustments, selecting and discarding memory blockers and hypnotic sedatives from the huge list of mind-altering drugs. Her aim was to create something unique—a long-lasting powerful drug that wouldn't damage the subject's body, but would remain effective without the constant need for reprogramming.

It was grueling work and often frustrating. But, in addition to being brilliant, Merlynn was very patient. In high school, she continued getting top grades without exerting any effort and spent most of her energy refining and testing the formula. Her parents and the local pharmacist, proud of the remarkable girl's cancer-fighting research, always cooperated.

When their only child was accepted at Harvard on full scholarship, Merlynn's parents had been ecstatic. But in college, she quickly became bored with her assigned experiments and decided to concentrate on her mind-control formula. Knowing she was close to achieving her goal, Merlynn cut classes and spent all her time in the lab. When she went home to Nevada for spring recess in her freshman year, she had just perfected her formula.

Merlynn's parents were furious with her. The university had alerted them that she wasn't attending class and they couldn't understand why. The visit quickly became unpleasant.

"You've got a free education at a wonderful school and you're blowing it!" her father had screamed.

Merlynn had tried to explain her need to experiment on her own, but this time, her mother and father both refused to listen.

The next day, she learned about the mine. She hadn't meant to eavesdrop, but her father was in the den with the door open, talking loudly on the phone, and practically jumping up and down in excitement.

"It's loaded with gold!" he had shouted. "Really? You're sure? How much?...Millions!"

Merlynn had entered the room after the phone call ended and sweetly pumped her father for information. Delighted by her interest, he proudly told her all the details. He had purchased one of the old abandoned mines in Elko County for practically nothing. And he had literally struck gold. The geologist he had been talking to on the phone had done extensive testing and discovered the mine had gold ore—lots of it—at least thirty years worth of production, maybe much more.

"We're going to be rich, Merlynn—very, very rich!" he had said, hugging his daughter and twirling her around the room.

Merlynn had smiled, danced with him, and pretended to share his excitement. And she was genuinely happy, but not for her father. She already had her own plan in mind.

Merlynn had tested her final formula two times. The first subject was her college roommate. She had slipped a small amount of the mixture into the girl's coffee-filled mug one evening and Hayley had immediately fallen asleep on top of her bed. While she slept, Merlynn watched the girl and occasionally spoke softly to her.

When Hayley woke up, she had asked Merlynn what had happened.

"You got very tired," Merlynn had explained. "Said you were going to sleep and you were out for ten hours. How do you feel now?"

"Fine," Hayley had said. Then, smiling at Merlynn, she had taken off her clothes and run through the dorm hallway completely naked.

That afternoon, Merlynn had again mixed a small dose of her drug into Hayley's drink. The girl didn't fall asleep this time, but listened attentively as Merlynn gave her another order. An hour later, with Merlynn watching, Hayley urinated into a cup, smiled sweetly, and then calmly drank her urine.

Merlynn continued adding her formula to Hayley's drinks for several more days, making the girl do whatever she wanted her to do, including performing sexual acts. (Merlynn had always been attracted to females rather than males—and Hayley was an extremely pretty blonde.)

But Merlynn hadn't been able to fully test her power over her roommate. When another dorm resident questioned whether Hayley was behaving strangely, Merlynn knew it was time to end the experiment. Reluctantly, after a final passionate tryst, she had released Hayley from her control.

Merlynn needed another subject—one that wouldn't arouse suspicion—so, this time, the person had to be a stranger. Her second test had required a bit of playacting. Merlynn had dressed like a hooker—black mini-skirt and black gloves—and gone to a bar in town where she quickly picked up an older man. She had been much thinner then, an attractive green-eyed girl with long curly brown hair, which she had covered that night with a blonde wig.

She had taken the man to a nearby cheap motel and, in the room, suggested they have a drink first. Still wearing her gloves, she had removed a bottle of wine from her shoulder bag, filled two glasses, and watched as the guy took several long sips. He had immediately fallen asleep.

While the man slept, she had whispered to him. When he awoke twelve hours later, he had stared blankly at Merlynn, who handed him a full bottle of Tylenol. Then, after giving him instructions, she had smiled and quietly left the room and the motel.

Two days later, she had read a small news article about a man found dead of an overdose in that seedy motel. The clerk had remembered him checking in with a young blonde-haired woman, whom the police never found.

During her visit home on spring break, it had been easy for Merlynn to use the formula again. The day following her discussion with her father about the gold mine, she had tucked a small liquid-filled vial into her jeans as she joined her parents for Saturday's breakfast. Then, after smiling and wishing them both a good morning, she had snuck a dose into their coffee mugs, and they had fallen asleep in their chairs.

As her mother and father tumbled onto the floor, Merlynn simply stepped around their bodies and ignored them for the rest of the day, although she did return at the optimum time to whisper instructions.

When her parents had finally awoken many hours later, they had been confused to find themselves sprawled on the kitchen floor. But Merlynn had been in the kitchen too, pretending to have also fallen asleep there.

"It must have been something we ate or drank," Merlynn had said, somewhat truthfully. "But it looks like we're all okay now." Of course, that remark had been a complete lie.

The next day, her mother and father had gone to church while Merlynn stayed home, complaining of a bad headache. But her parents had never reached their destination. Instead, their car, traveling at eighty miles an hour, had smashed into a tree, killing both of them instantly. For some reason, her father's foot had been on the accelerator, leading the police to theorize the man may have had a heart attack and lost consciousness before the crash. In any event, Merlynn's parents were dead and the town grieved for the poor girl who was now an orphan.

Merlynn had forced herself to wait until the day after her parents' funeral to contact Lance Kimbrough, the geologist. Since the man wasn't local, he hadn't heard about the accident. After identifying herself, she had explained the reason for her call.

"My parents were killed in a car crash last Sunday morning," she had said, speaking in a quivery voice filled with sadness.

"Oh, I'm so sorry," Kimbrough had replied. "I didn't know your mother and only knew your father a short time. But he seemed like a very nice man. In fact, I just spoke to him last week."

Merlynn had feigned surprise. "Really? I had no idea. I called you because I was going through his papers and found some information about a mine he owned along with your name and number." It had been difficult for her to maintain an appropriately solemn tone. "What's this all about?"

He had confirmed the good news, adding specific details about the size and location of the gold bonanza.

It's true—I'm really gonna be a millionaire! she had thought, suppressing shrieks of joy. Then she had again assumed her somber tone. "Have you told anyone else about the discovery?" she had asked.

"No."

"Keep it that way, please."

"Sure."

After several more probing questions, she had ended the call and smiled. Even without meeting Lance Kimbrough, she knew the geologist was a loner, whose only interest in life was rocks and minerals. She had been confident he would keep his news to himself. And she had been right.

Merlynn grinned at the happy memories as her mind returned to the present. She stuffed another cupcake into her mouth and rose, leaning both arms on the desk for balance.

"Woman 3, come here!" she shouted.

Immediately, a pale blonde teenager, wearing a shift dress that was much too big for her scrawny body, rushed up to Merlynn and bowed her head.

"To the bedroom," Merlynn ordered. "You'll help me with my bath and clothes."

With the girl holding her hand, the obese woman waddled out of her office into the wide corridor. It was time to prepare for the evening's performance.

At eight o'clock Sunday evening, Merlynn pressed the button behind her desk that turned on the televisions in the living rooms of the occupied houses of Corsonia. "Men and women," she announced from her regal chair as Dugan operated the hand-held camera. "It is time to listen to me." After waiting a minute for her audience to assemble, she began.

"I have some new instructions for the coming days." She picked up two sheets of paper from the desk and glanced at the first one. "Man 33, you will not go on the bus to the mine anymore. Instead, at seven a.m. tomorrow morning, you will use the truck to load the water bottles from the store and deliver them to all the houses. You will also pick up the empty bottles from every house and bring them back to me. Then, when I am ready, you will pick up the filled bottles and bring them to the store. Man 40, you will take the bus to the mine tomorrow.

"Now moving to another topic..." Merlynn turned to the second paper and read from the sheet. "Woman 21, for the next seven nights, you will have sex with Man 43. Woman 8, you will have sex with Man 27. Woman 12, you will have sex with Man 33 and Woman 17, you will have sex with Man 15—also for the next seven nights." She placed the paper on the desk and smiled at her unseen audience. "We really need you people to produce more children."

Merlynn folded her hands together and stared at the camera, her expression now serious. "My next message is for all men and all women. I have just discovered that we have intruders in Corsonia, two teenage girls who are driving a silver car. They want to hurt all of you. The intruders have been seen near the boys' school, so Boys' Teacher and Woman 28, you must be especially aware of these dangerous girls. As soon as any of you see them, this is what you must do..."

CHAPTER 10

After parking the car among the rocks early Monday afternoon, Loren and Tracie walked to their usual spot behind the schoolhouse to wait for Boy 11.

"I hope this works," Tracie said as she sat on the pebbly lawn. "Then we'll head to the boys' house and do the same thing there."

"It's the first step." After removing her heavy backpack, Loren knelt near Tracie. "I just hope he's gonna be able to make the switch."

"We don't have much time left before the full moon on Friday so we've gotta move fast."

"Yeah, I..."

"Hello."

The girls turned and smiled at Boy 11.

"How do you always do that—sneak up behind us?" Loren asked.

"I do not know," he replied seriously. The boy wore a pair of navy shorts, still much too big for him, and an enormous gray tee shirt with the words "The X-Files" emblazoned in bold black lettering.

"Boy 11, we have something important for you to do today that'll help you and the other boys," Loren said, smiling as she grabbed the backpack, opened it, and pointed to four unmarked bottles of water. "You've gotta take these and put them in the refrigerator here. Then take all the bottles of water that are in the refrigerator and throw them away. Do you think you can do that?"

The boy's eyes widened with fear. "It is forbidden for us to touch the water bottles."

"We know," Tracie said softly. "But we really need you to do this."

He shook his head.

Before the girls could convince the frightened boy to exchange the bottles, they all heard a door of the schoolhouse slam shut. When they turned toward the noise, they saw a balding bearded man, the bottom of his hair tied together, and a woman with a white ponytail, heading toward them.

"What's going on?" Loren asked as she quickly closed the backpack, lifted it onto her shoulders, and stared at the rapidly approaching pair.

"Look!" Tracie shouted, pointing at the twosome. "They've got knives! Run!" She tried to link arms with Boy 11, who stood mesmerized by the approaching couple. The man and woman each held a large carving knife as they continued their methodical forward march. With their robot-like strides, the pair was now only a few yards away—and closing in quickly.

"I cannot leave," Boy 11 said, pushing away Tracie's arm.

Loren and Tracie turned and ran as rapidly as they could toward the car. But Loren's progress was slowed by the heavy water-filled backpack.

"C'mon," Tracie said, urging her friend to move faster.

The girls heard a thump as a large rock flew over their heads and landed in front of them. That noise was immediately followed by a series of small clinking sounds as a cascade of pebbles fell to their right.

"Ow!" Tracie yelled as several stones landed on her leg.

"Oh, yeah? Take this!" Loren lifted a large rock and tossed it at the attackers. The stone landed in front of the long-faced blank-eyed woman, who, without a pause, stepped over it and continued advancing toward them.

"She didn't even blink," Loren said, trying to run faster. A rock flew over her left shoulder, missing her body by just a few inches. "They're getting closer!"

Tracie bent down and picked up an enormous rock. "Here," she said. "Help me throw this."

Together, the two girls tossed the boulder at their pursuers and it fell directly in their path. As the man and woman maneuvered around the obstacle, Loren and Tracie gained enough space to move out of rock-throwing range. They ran quickly, stumbling the last few yards toward the car.

"Let's get out of here!" Tracie yelled as she and Loren jumped into the Prius.

After Loren locked the doors and turned on the ignition, they both heard a loud thump.

Tracie turned and stared at the scene behind them. "They're throwing rocks at the car!" she shouted. "Move it!" As she watched, the man rushed toward them, his carving knife aimed at the rear tire while the woman picked up a fistful of pebbles.

"Now!" Tracie yelled and the car sped forward, accompanied by the crackling sound of shattered glass.

"What just broke?" Loren asked as she veered the car onto the county road.

"The back window on your side. Did any of the glass hit you?"

"I don't think so...Shit, I'm still shaking. Help me get this backpack off. I don't want to stop the car in case those two zombie creeps are still chasing us."

"They may act like robots, but they can't outrun a car," Tracie said as she helped her friend wriggle free of the backpack. "You should've just left this back at the school."

"Uh uh. I don't want them to find the water and know what we were doing."

"What about Boy 11? He knows."

"We just gotta hope he won't tell them."

Loren continued driving and the girls sat quietly until Tracie spoke. "What the hell happened back there?"

"Whoever's doing this must've found out about us. And obviously, they don't want us around."

"Who were those zombie robots?"

"Probably the housekeeper for the school, I think Boy 11 said her name was Woman 28, and the man must've been the teacher."

"Some teacher."

"Yeah. But someone told them to attack us. It's like they're programmed."

"So we gotta figure out who's programming those people."

"And we gotta help Boy 11," Loren said. "He wouldn't come with us and that man and woman know he was out there talking to us."

"They knew that before. When we talked to him, we were always out in the open. We weren't hiding from them."

"That was before they were ordered to go after us, when they didn't care. Now they care."

"What do you think they're gonna do to Boy 11?"

Loren shook her head. "Nothing good, that's for sure."

CHAPTER 11

"What were you talking about with those two girls today?" Merlynn asked Boy 11. She sat in her office behind her massive desk, speaking calmly and quietly.

The frightened boy stood in front of Merlynn, his head bowed, but didn't answer. He had never been in a building of this size—or seen a woman like this. In addition to her enormous girth, she spoke and acted differently than the grownups he was used to dealing with.

"Answer the question." Her voice was now louder and more demanding.

Boy 11 stared at the strange woman before speaking. "They asked me about school," he whispered.

"What did they want to know?"

"They wanted to know what I learned."

"And you told them?"

"Yes."

Merlynn picked up a book from her desk and waved it at the boy. "What about this? Where'd you get it?"

Boy 11 looked at the cover of *Swiss Family Robinson* and lowered his head again. "They gave it to me," he whispered.

"Why?"

"I asked for a book to read."

"And the girls just gave it to you?"

The boy nodded.

"What nice friends you have. What're their names?"

"I do not know," he lied.

"Really? You never asked them their names?"

"No."

Merlynn leaned against her chair and considered his answer. *Possible*, she thought. The kid was just a number himself so maybe people's names weren't important to him.

"How many times did you talk to them?"

"I do not remember."

"Once? Twice? Ten times?"

"I may have talked to them two times or perhaps three times. I am not sure."

"Did the girls ever talk about where they lived or what they were doing here?"

"No."

"They just asked about you? Did you mention you were finishing school soon?" She glanced at a paper on the desk. "On Friday, in fact."

"No."

"I don't believe you!" she shouted. "You must've talked about that." Unfortunately, she couldn't use a truth serum on him; it negated the effects of her mind-control drug and the combination was usually lethal, especially with children.

Merlynn scowled at the boy, who now cowered in front of her, shaking visibly. "All right. We're through talking." She stood up, resting her arms on the desk, and smiled sweetly at the distraught boy. "You're going to have an early graduation—Man 24, come in here now!"

A tall and thin ponytailed bearded man in his late thirties, limping slightly, immediately entered the office. He wore torn jeans and an oversized tee shirt and stared blankly at Merlynn.

"Take the boy to my laboratory," she ordered. "Get him ready."

Boy 11 whimpered as the man grasped his arms and pushed him toward the door. "Please," he begged, turning to face Merlynn, tears rimming his eyes. "I have done nothing wrong."

She shook her head. "Sorry, kid, but you're too smart and curious for my needs. And I sure can't have you running around loose, talking to strangers."

"I will not talk to them anymore."

"Yeah, right," she chuckled, reaching for the ever-present box of Hostess cupcakes on her desk. "What's the big difference? You were going to finish school on Friday anyway, so it would've happened then." She grabbed a cupcake, tore off the cellophane wrapping, and took a hefty bite. "It's just a couple of days sooner." As she spoke, a dab of cream filling coated the corner of her lower lip. "You won't even remember."

With a wave of her hefty hand, Merlynn signaled that the discussion was over. While she finished chewing, the man dragged the teary-eyed boy out of her office. After dabbing her mouth with a tissue, she lifted herself out of her chair and slowly followed them.

Merlynn's laboratory occupied a mammoth sunlit room a half-flight up the end of a lengthy hallway. Cluttered shelves and counters lined three of the walls. Some were filled with intricate pipe arrangements, while others housed various jars and bottles filled with powders and liquids. An assortment of odd-looking machines and test tubes covered a huge worktable. The fourth wall—featuring floor-to-ceiling windows—jutted high above the ground, overlooking the picturesque hilly landscape.

By the time Merlynn entered the lab, Boy 11 already sat upright in what looked like the patient's chair of a dental office, positioned in the middle of the room. Man 24, using both of his arms, held the frightened boy in place.

"What are you going to do to me?" Boy 11 whispered as the obese woman waddled toward him.

"Nothing that will hurt," she said, smiling. "You must be thirsty by now so I'm just going to give you something to drink."

"A bottle of water?"

"If you'd like." She reached for a bottle of clear liquid and held it in front of his face. "Or you can have something else. Would you rather drink milk or orange juice? I'm really very accommodating." She smiled again.

Boy 11 shook his head and tried to keep his mouth closed.

"Open it," Merlynn ordered and Man 24 immediately forced the boy's lips and teeth apart. She unscrewed the bottle cap and poured a few ounces of water into Boy 11's throat.

"Swallow," she said. "If you don't, I'll keep pouring water into your mouth anyway. You'll gag, maybe throw up, and it'll just take that much longer. Trust me, it's better if you cooperate."

Boy 11 stared at the woman and then swallowed the water.

Man 24 held the boy's mouth open again and Merlynn poured more water into it. As she repeated the procedure a third time, the boy closed his eyes and water dribbled down his chin.

Merlynn adjusted the chair's setting into a horizontal position and waved her hand, dismissing Man 24. Then she gazed at the sleeping boy and grinned. "Have a good long rest, kid. I'll be in to visit you later."

Just after midnight, Merlynn, wearing a tent-like flower-patterned nightgown, returned by herself to the laboratory. Enough light from the nearly full moon streamed into the heavily windowed room so, without turning on a lamp, she was able to discern Boy 11, still sleeping soundly, exactly as she had left him.

"Okay," she said, dragging a swivel chair next to the boy and sitting in it. "It's time for you to listen. I am Merlynn, your leader, and, whenever you hear my voice, you will immediately do what I say. Do you understand?"

Without opening his eyes, Boy 11 nodded.

"You are no longer named Boy 11. Your name is now Man 4 and you will answer only to the name Man 4. Do you understand?"

The boy nodded.

"What is your name?"

"My name is Man 4," he whispered, his eyes still shut.

"Who is Boy 11?"

"I do not know."

"Very good. You are a quick learner. All right. You are now a man. You will no longer live with the boys and go to school. You will live with the other men and go to work. When you wake up, you will wait for me to give you further instructions. Do you understand?"

"Yes."

"Once again, what is your name?"

"My name is Man 4."

"Who is the only person you will now listen to?

"I will only listen to you."

"And you will do whatever I tell you to do?"

"Yes."

Merlynn smiled and patted the boy's hand. "You may continue to sleep, Man 4. I will talk to you again when you wake up."

CHAPTER 12

Lance Kimbrough stood at the entrance to the mine early Tuesday morning and waited as the workers finished changing into their mining outfits, grabbed their headgear, and formed rows, ready to begin their daily duties. As he checked off their numbers, the men and women took their lunchboxes and headed toward the shaft.

The numbers had bothered him at first. "Why are they using numbers instead of names?" he had asked Merlynn.

"It's easier to keep track of everyone," she had explained. "Besides, why does it matter? The miners don't care what they're called as long as they get paid."

The geologist called a new number he had just been given, "Man 4," and a thin blond-haired boy—not even old enough to be a teenager—responded.

"Here," the boy said.

"You haven't been in the mine before, have you?" Kimbrough asked.

"No."

He gazed at the boy's calm demeanor. "Are you sure you want to do this kind of work? Did anyone force you to come here?"

"I want to work in the mine," Man 4 said. "I was not forced to come here."

This boy was the third young person to join his workforce in the last few months. After the second child, Kimbrough had questioned Merlynn about the ages of the new workers.

"You know that the kids in this town are all home-schooled," she had told him. "They finish school early and they don't want to go on to college—or even high school. They'd rather make lots of money in the mine."

It's true about the money, Kimbrough thought. He paid these people big bucks—in cash—each week. But when did they have a chance to spend their earnings? They worked here seven days a week. The geologist chuckled. *What the heck?* He never took any days off either, spending all his time at the mine. There was nothing he enjoyed doing more.

He glanced at the workers. They always seemed so focused on their jobs. They never talked much, even to each other. Maybe they were like him and enjoyed the mining work too. In any case, he wasn't big about interacting with people so their no-nonsense attitude suited him well. He told them what to do, they listened, and then they did what they were told. They always did what they were told.

"I don't know about this." Tracie shook her head as Loren drove from their motel toward Corsonia after breakfast Tuesday.

"We've gotta try to get to their house and switch the water," Loren said. "The full moon's on Friday and then Boy 11's done with school."

"But they caught him with us yesterday and we don't know what's happened to him. Maybe he's not in school anymore."

"Yeah, I know. I hope he's okay and still there." Loren stopped talking and the girls sat quietly for several minutes.

"What if those zombies come after us again?" Tracie finally asked.

"We're ready for them this time."

"Not really," Tracie grumbled.

"Well, anyway, they'll be looking for us in a silver Prius, not in this car." Loren had convinced Montello's only used car dealer to let her rent a forest green Jeep for the week, hoping a different vehicle would confuse their pursuers. Also, the Jeep had four-wheel drive, which would help them navigate the rough terrain. If her mother ever questioned the move, Loren planned to claim the Prius had needed work, which was true. It did need a new driver's-side rear window.

"This time, I'm gonna get off past where we usually go," Loren said. "The tire marks probably led them to us." She swerved off the road and drove about ten feet before she stopped the Jeep and turned to Tracie. "C'mon. Help me wipe off these new tracks so no one can see them."

After the girls smoothed out the rocky ground with their sneakers, they returned to the car and Loren drove quickly past the schoolhouse toward the boys' home.

"We can't just leave the Jeep here where anyone can see it and walk up over the hill to the house like we did before," Tracie said as Loren parked the car behind the largest grouping of rocks.

"We don't have much of a choice."

"But there's no place to hide between here and the house—and, if you remember, last time we ran into those robot-people, they were carrying knives."

"Well, this time, we've got knives too—and our secret weapon," Loren said, patting the can of Mace that stuck out of her jeans pocket.

Tracie shook her head. "I don't know. We'd have to be real close to those weirdos—too close—to use those little steak knives, or even the pepper spray. Besides, I don't think I could stab someone."

"Maybe we won't have to do anything. Maybe it'll be like last time and the house'll be empty."

"You think?"

Loren shrugged.

Without further conversation, the girls climbed to the top of the incline, dropped to the ground, and looked at the building below.

"Shit," Loren mumbled.

In front of the brown house at the bottom of the hill stood two bearded men with ponytails. And both of them carried rifles.

"Okay, bold leader, what do you suggest we do now?" Tracie whispered as she lay on the rocky ground and studied the two men below.

"Shh. Let me think."

The girls watched the bearded men for a couple of minutes.

"They're not even moving or anything," Loren finally whispered. "Maybe we could circle around quietly behind them and go into the back of the house and open the sliding glass door like we did last time."

"No. First of all, there could be other guards behind the house waiting for us. Also, whoever's in charge knows that we've been checking around here and talking to Boy 11 so they must've fixed the lock." Shaking her head, Tracie began sliding her body backwards. "We can't stay. The Jeep's exposed and we don't know where that mean sheriff is. Those guys down there might be zombies, but he's definitely not. C'mon."

"Damn," Loren muttered as she hurried with Tracie toward the car. "We're running out of time if we want to help Boy 11 and Boy 12—and everyone else here. We've gotta find another way to get in."

"I'm gonna stop at the school," Loren said as she drove away from the boys' house.

"They'll be looking for us there too."

"I know. But I just want to make sure Boy 11's okay. It's our fault if something's happened to him." Loren glanced at Tracie. "Listen, I'm gonna get out and look for him. But you stay in the car, sit in the driver's seat, and keep the motor running so if one of those crazy zombies comes after me, I can just jump in and we can take off."

"What if those weirdos have guns this time instead of knives?"

"Since all I've got is the Mace, I better be able to move fast."

Tracie shook her head. "I don't like it, Lor, but you're not gonna listen to me anyway. Where am I waiting in the car? Not in a driveway across the street. That's too far for you to run if those robots start shooting at you."

"You're right. I'm gonna drive into the yard next to the laundry line. That'll hide it a little from the road."

"Not very much—and anyone in the house can see the car from the back windows."

"I'm still hoping they've been told to look for a silver Prius—not a green Jeep. And remember, these people don't seem to be able to think for themselves."

"Yeah. But they've also been told to look for us—and we're not disguised."

"We won't stay very long, just enough to check on Boy 11." Loren reached the boys' school and pulled the car behind the clothesline, which was full of shirts and shorts. "Okay. Here we are." She ran out of the Jeep, leaving the car running and Tracie slid into the vacated driver's seat.

Almost immediately, a door in the schoolhouse slammed shut and a boy rushed toward Loren. But it wasn't Boy 11.

"You must leave," Boy 12 said, gasping for breath. "They are going to hurt you."

"Where's Boy 11?" Loren asked.

"I do not know. They took him away and he did not return."

"Do you have any idea where they took him?"

Boy 12 shook his head. "He did not sleep in the room last night. His clothes are gone. I will be next." The boy looked sadly at Loren, tears filling his dark brown eyes.

"Please come with us," Loren begged. "Don't go back inside. If they see you talking to me, they could take you too."

The boy shook his head and backed away. Then he turned and raced to the school.

At that moment, a door slammed shut and the same zombie-like man and woman who had attacked Loren and Tracie the previous day, ran toward Loren. She opened the passenger door, stepped inside, and rolled down the window. "I promise we'll find Boy 11 and we'll help both of you—and all the other boys," she shouted. "I promise!"

As Loren leaned out of the window yelling her final promise, the ponytailed man and woman, again holding carving knives, neared the car. The blank-eyed woman raised her right arm and tossed a blade at Loren's head. The girl ducked and the knife made a thumping sound as it hit the roof of the Jeep and bounced onto the ground.

As the woman's companion swung his knife at the car's tires, Loren grabbed her can of Mace and sprayed it at the man's expressionless face. Without speaking, he immediately released the weapon and placed his hands over his injured eyes.

"Go!" Loren shouted.

Tracie pressed her foot on the accelerator and steered the Jeep toward the county road.

"You do know that we can't go back to the school anymore," Tracie said a few minutes later as she drove toward the motel. "Right now, we're hurting those kids, not helping them. Boy 11's already missing, thanks to us, and, after today, Boy 12 could be in trouble too."

"Hmm."

"Did you hear what I just said?"

Loren looked at Tracie and nodded. "Yeah, I heard you. I know we haven't helped the boys yet. But we will."

"How can you be so sure? None of your plans have worked so far and we're lucky we haven't been killed by those zombie people. Do you agree that we can't go back to the school?"

"Yeah."

"And we shouldn't go to the house either. We can't get around those guards."

"Okay."

Tracie glanced quickly at her friend. "How come you're agreeing with everything I say? You never do that."

"Because you're right. Also, going to the house and school's not gonna tell us anything new. We've gotta find out who's behind all of this and it's gotta have something to do with that mine. Who's the owner? That's what I want to check."

"Maybe it's the sheriff. He's the only one here who's acted normal, even if he was mean to us."

"Nah. I don't think so. He didn't seem smart enough to be in charge. I think he's working for someone."

"Well, maybe we should check him out anyway."

"How? We don't even know his name."

"Yeah, but he said he's the sheriff. If he is, shouldn't he be listed as an officer for the town?"

"Maybe. Lemme try to look up 'Corsonia.'" Loren took her phone from her jeans pocket and turned it on. "Still no service here," she said, shaking her head. "But back in Montello, we can do some research, find out more about the sheriff, the town—and that mine."

The girls were quiet as Tracie continued driving. "What do you think they've done to Boy 11?" she finally asked.

"I don't know. But it's nothing good."

"Do you think they've hurt him?" Tracie whispered. "Or worse?"

"I hope not. Remember what he told us about that other boy who disappeared and then he saw again?"

"The one who didn't know who Boy 11 was? I think his name was Boy 2."

"Yeah. But from what Boy 11 told us, the kid didn't recognize that name anymore."

Tracie glanced at Loren. "If they've done something like that to Boy 11 to turn him into a zombie, then he won't know who we are either, so how can we even help him?"

"I don't know," Loren said. "But we've got to find him first."

"There's not much information here on Corsonia," Loren told Tracie as she sat cross-legged on her bed in their Montello motel room checking her phone. "According to the last census in 2010, it's a teeny town with a population of just 26."

"That can't be right. We saw those three buses at the mine so there's gotta be more than a hundred people living there."

"Well, they're not being counted, probably because somebody doesn't want them to be. Probably the same somebody who's turning them into zombies."

Tracie leaned on her elbows on the other bed. "What about the name of the sheriff?" she asked.

"No sheriff listed. There's just a mayor, 'John Smith.'" Loren smirked. "That name sounds phony to me."

"Is there anything about a mine in Corsonia?"

"Lemme check." Loren tried googling "mines in Corsonia," "Corsonia gold mine," and "Corsonia silver mine." She shrugged. "Not much here either. All I get is one sentence: 'A small gold mine in Corsonia, Nevada opened in 1897 and closed in 1913.'"

"So it must've run out of gold then."

"Yeah," Loren agreed. "But now it's open again, with at least three busloads of people working there. Hey, Trace, do you think that's where Boy 11 is?"

"It's possible."

"Then I think we should go back and check the mine."

"Are you nuts?" Tracie shouted. "That place is in the middle of nowhere, but it still has a fence all around to keep people away. Now that they know about us, they'll have guards posted everywhere. Besides, even if Boy 11's there, if he's been turned into a zombie, he won't know who we are. We got away from two robot people with knives—but we can't fight a hundred of them."

"We have to find out more about the mine and who's running it and we can't learn anything from here." Loren smiled at her friend. "I've got another plan."

Tracie rolled her eyes, fell backwards onto her pillow, and sighed.

CHAPTER 13

"My beard itches," Tracie complained as Loren drove the Jeep toward Corsonia Wednesday before dawn.

"That's nothing compared to what's covering my face," Loren said with a chuckle, pointing to her much longer and thicker dark blonde beard.

"What if we can't get these stupid things off after gluing them on? We'll both have to join the circus."

"Yeah, well you've just got the short beard. I'm the one who's the real bearded lady. Anyway, the directions said it'll come off easy with cold cream."

"Even if the hair comes off, we're both gonna get zits," Tracie said, gently stroking her chin. "This dumb idea better work. Otherwise, if whoever's doing all this finds us, we're gonna be zombies too."

"They won't unless the robot teacher and housekeeper told them about the new car—and I'm figuring they didn't."

"You mean you're hoping."

"Trace, those people don't even talk."

"They talk if they're asked a question."

"Well, you think someone asked, 'Did those girls have a new car?'"

Tracie shrugged.

"So as I was saying," Loren continued, "I figure they're still looking for two girls in a silver Prius, not two men in a green Jeep. With our beards and hair in ponytails, this disguise should be good enough to fool them. And they're not gonna see the car 'cause it's green and we're gonna shove it deep into the bushes."

"We don't know anything about working in a mine, Lor. What about the clothes they wear—and that helmet with the lamp on it?"

"The man we saw getting on the bus at the boys' house was just carrying a lunch pail—and we've each got that, filled with our own food and water. The other equipment's gotta be at the mine so we can put it on there."

"You better be right about all this."

"It's the only way to find out what's going on," Loren said as she veered off the main road and headed toward the mine.

As Loren drove past the boys' school, Tracie began reading from the directions she had scribbled on their earlier trip. "I hope this works...See the big yellow bush coming up? There should be a dirt road on the left that you have to turn into. Yes! Turn here."

With Tracie giving instructions, Loren continued driving until she reached the wooded hill leading to the mine and followed it to the top. "There's the gated entrance," Loren said. "I'm gonna drive off the road and park in the back near the hole in the fence." She swung the Jeep through the bushy terrain and steered it along the perimeter of the fence.

"You're getting this rental car full of scratches," Tracie complained.

"I'll pay for them. I don't care." After driving halfway around the circular fence, Loren guided the Jeep into a clump of the tallest shrubs. "See?" she said smugly, after they both stepped out and examined the camouflaged vehicle. "I was right. You can hardly see the car."

"Then how're we gonna remember where the Jeep is if it's dark when we come back?"

"Good point. Let's get something that'll help us find it." Loren looked at the nearby bushes and smiled. "Here." She darted to a cropping of rubber rabbitbrush, tore off a handful of the flowering yellow blossoms, and tossed them several feet in front of where the Jeep was hidden. "Even in the dark, with our flashlights, we should be able to see this."

Tracie nodded. "I guess now we're up to the next step."

"Yup. Let's get started."

Loren and Tracie found the piece of brown paper still wedged into the fence. After pushing apart the opening at the bottom, they crawled through and readjusted the barrier. Then, walking quietly, they circled back toward the locked gate and hid behind the bushes near the empty parking lot.

A few minutes later they heard the sounds of an approaching engine and, as they continued to watch, the first yellow bus drove into the lot. The door opened and about thirty people stepped out, all wearing jeans and carrying lunch pails. The group included men with long beards and tied-back hair; women, all with similar long ponytails, none of them wearing makeup; and one young teenage boy.

"Not Boy 11," Loren whispered.

"No. But maybe it's the one he met who'd changed, who used to be Boy 2, or the other one, Boy 9."

"Yeah," Loren agreed. "Okay. Let's go."

As the people began walking down the hill, staring straight ahead and not talking, Loren and Tracie dashed behind the last man and marched with them, trying to mimic their long strides and blank expressions.

When the workers reached the mine complex at the bottom of

the hill, they all entered a nearby brown shack. The girls followed them into a large windowless room illuminated by a single light bulb. Three huge open bins occupied most of the space—one with blue jumpsuits, another with boots, and the third with lighted helmets. As Loren and Tracie watched, the robotic people grabbed jumpsuits, stepped into the swinging-door booths, changed into the mining uniforms, shoved their clothes into numbered cubbies on the other side of the room, put on boots and helmets, and exited.

With a nod to each other, the girls quickly grabbed jumpsuits, changed into them, wriggled into the rubber boots, donned helmets, and tossed their tops and jeans in one of the few unnumbered cubbies. Then, racing out of the building, they joined the rest of the bus group, who had gathered around the mine entrance, forming several rows near the opening. All the people stood still.

"What are they waiting for?" Tracie whispered.

"Shh. I don't know. Maybe the others?"

"This uniform smells real bad," Tracie continued. "It's gross wearing someone else's dirty clothes."

"Shut up. You'll shower later."

The workers continued to stand quietly for several minutes, not speaking or looking at anyone. Then Loren and Tracie heard the sounds of approaching footsteps and a second group of people silently formed additional rows behind them. They waited again until a third group joined the assembly.

At that point, a thin man with glasses and a short goatee, carrying a clipboard, walked to the entrance. "Good morning," he said, smiling. "It's good to see you all again. Are you ready to work?"

"Yes," most of the people mumbled or muttered.

Tracie poked Loren and pointed to the man with the clipboard.

Loren held her finger to her lips.

"Then let's get started," the man said, glancing at his clipboard. "Man 1?"

"Here," a monotone voice replied and a young man in his mid

twenties with a long scraggly beard and ponytail stepped forward and continued into the mine.

"Man 2?"

A young teen, not much older than Boy 11, moved through the rows of people and raised his hand. "Here," he said in a high squeaky voice.

The man with the clipboard checked off the name and smiled at the boy as he entered the mine.

"Man 3?"

Another bearded and ponytailed man in his middle twenties acknowledged the number and entered the mine.

"Man 4?"

Both girls recognized Boy 11 as he said, "Here," stepped through the lines, and followed the others inside the mine.

"No..." Loren mumbled.

Tracie shook her head, moving her index finger to her bearded mouth.

As the man with the clipboard continued calling the names of the males—in sequence, with only a few numbers missing—Loren grasped Tracie's hand and, slowly, the two girls backed themselves out of the group.

None of the waiting workers acknowledged their movements. Instead, the group continued to stand quietly at attention, listening for their names as the man with the clipboard read from his sheet.

"What now?" Tracie whispered, when they were out of the clipboard man's view. "We're not on his list and soon he's gonna be finished with the men's numbers."

"We have to find a moment when he's not looking and sneak inside."

"Lor, he's not one of these zombies. He doesn't have the ponytail and he acts like a real person, like the sheriff. Maybe he's even the one who's controlling these people."

"I don't think so. He seems much too wimpy. We're gonna rush in before he sees us. Just follow my lead."

The girls returned to the group, working their way into the aisle of the row closest to the mine's entrance. They watched as the man with the clipboard read the next number.

"Man 41," he called.

"Here." A burly red-haired man in his fifties with a frizzy beard and ponytail stepped forward.

"Good," the man with the clipboard said. Then, glancing at his feet, he dropped his clipboard on the ground and bent down to tie the laces on one of his sneakers.

Loren immediately darted inside the entrance of the mineshaft with Tracie right behind her. As they leaned against the side of the stone cavern, they heard the man speak.

"Okay. Now where was I?...Man 42."

Carrying lunch pails, Loren and Tracie switched on their headlamps and followed several of the silent men along the dark corridor, their helmets lighting the way. Then the workers all stopped and stood silently around an opening in the shaft.

Tracie poked Loren in the ribs. When her friend looked at her, Tracie shrugged, spreading her hands in a questioning motion.

Loren pointed to an elevator, rising eerily from the lower depths of the mine.

When the elevator reached the top level and opened, Tracie stared at it with horror. The "elevator" was more like a cage, a rickety wooden structure with heavy slats along its sides. It didn't resemble any elevator she'd ever been in. *Maybe a service elevator in an old apartment building, like in the movies.* She didn't feel any better after stepping inside the shaky contraption. The cage rattled and groaned as it dropped, making her even more nervous.

Finally, the elevator slowed and then abruptly stopped. The door opened and Tracie and Loren were greeted by a blast of oppressively hot air as they entered a dark—and noisy—cavern. Loud thumping and clanging sounds emanated from somewhere along the vast hallway to their right.

Again the two girls followed the workers, who placed their lunchboxes on a long table near the elevator and took safety goggles from a box on the floor. Next, as Loren and Tracie watched, the men strode through the black corridor in the direction of the noise, their helmets providing streams of light in front of them.

"Do you see any place we can leave our lunches so we don't get them mixed up with the others?" Loren whispered.

"Maybe in the corner here, on the floor." Tracie pointed to a spot near the table. "But take out a bottle of water first. It's hot here so we're gonna need it and we sure don't want to drink their stuff. C'mon, I hear the elevator door opening. More of them are gonna be coming."

After removing the unlabeled bottles and putting them in the pockets of their jumpsuits, they each grabbed a pair of safety glasses and scampered down the hallway toward the loud cacophonous sounds.

As she walked, Tracie tapped her beard. "This stupid disguise is really annoying," she whispered. "And it's gonna get all sweaty."

"Stop complaining, you wuss. I'm the one with the really long beard so, in this heat, it's much worse for me."

The girls continued along the corridor until they reached the area where many of the men were already working. A few held hand drills, but most of the miners pounded the rock wall with hammers and pickaxes. Even in the dim light, Loren and Tracie could see the sweat pouring from their expressionless faces.

The noise was nearly deafening. "What are we supposed to do here?" Tracie shouted into her friend's ear.

"Grab a hammer and get to work." Loren picked up one of the

tools, which lay in a bin near the wall, moved to an open area, and began attacking the stone surface. Then, copying the miners, she lifted the rocks she had dislodged from the wet ground and tossed them into a nearby chute.

Tracie took a hammer and joined her. "We can't do this all day," she yelled. "I'll pass out and fall on my bearded face."

"Just do a little and pretend that you're working. See if anyone's watching us." Loren waved Tracie to come nearer and spoke directly into her ear. "I want to find Boy 11 and question him. Maybe he can tell us something."

Tracie swung her hammer at the rock and then turned to Loren. "If he's one of them, he won't be able to," she said, enunciating each word so her friend would understand her.

"I still want to make sure. C'mon and follow what I do." Loren gestured with her hand as she hammered the rock once and then shimmied several feet to the left through the muddy water until she stood next to a short balding man with a gray beard and a thin ponytail who stared intently at the wall as he attacked it with his pickaxe.

Tracie copied Loren's motions.

Loren repeated her hammering and shimmying routine four times. Then she stopped, tapped Tracie's shoulder, and pointed to her left. Standing several feet from her, pounding his hammer at the stone and totally focused on his actions, was Boy 11.

After calling the number of the final woman miner, Lance Kimbrough left the shaft entrance to continue his daily duties. Without any skilled workers to help him, the geologist was also responsible for the blasting and refining. In fact, he was in charge of everything.

Although he loved the mine and his job, he was disappointed by Merlynn's lack of interest in any of his suggestions. In addition to a request for skilled employees, he had asked the owner to modernize the mine—install air conditioning, redo the old elevator, and provide haul trucks. But other than paying for a few jackleg drills, she had refused to do anything.

"People worked in this mine in the last century under these conditions so it'll be just fine for us," she had said. "No one's complaining."

When he had explained how much more efficiently the mine could operate, she had smiled and said, "I'm in no hurry."

He had also asked about complying with the state's environmental and regulatory controls, but she had immediately squelched the question.

"You just run the mine and let me handle the legal end," she had said.

And she wasn't concerned about the miners' safety either. "They'll be just fine," she had repeated.

Fortunately, the Corsonia mine was bolstered by solid stone so there was no chance of a collapse, but Kimbrough still worried about accidents. Without Merlynn's permission, and using his own money, he had bought safety goggles for the workers. And by leaving the goggles at the bottom of the mine, he was sure she'd never find out.

Kimbrough shrugged. The woman never even visited the mine complex. Although Dugan came by each week to pay the workers and pick up the refined ore, the sheriff rarely entered the shaft either. As long as gold kept being produced, Merlynn seemed to be satisfied.

After one last glance at the mine entrance, Kimbrough opened his office door and stepped inside.

"Hello!" Loren yelled to Boy 11.

There was no reaction. He continued to pound the rock wall

with his sledgehammer.

Between the whirring noise from the motorized drills and the clunking of the axes and hammers, it was nearly impossible to hear anything. Finally, Loren touched the boy's shoulder and he jumped back, staring at her in astonishment.

"It's okay," she mouthed, holding up her hands and waving them in front of him. "I just want to talk to you."

The boy shook his head and began hammering the wall again.

Loren turned to Tracie and shrugged. She reached into her jumpsuit pocket, took out her phone, and snapped a few photos of the miners, including Boy 11. None of them reacted to the sudden flashes of light. Then, picking up her hammer, she started pounding the wall, but at a much slower pace than the boy—about one stroke to every four of his.

Tracie joined in, banging at the rock occasionally, but mostly just holding her hammer next to the wall. She glanced in both directions to see if anyone was watching her, but all she saw was intense pounding by the workers around her, their eyes focused on the stone.

She felt a hand on her shoulder and turned toward Loren, who pointed to her watch, rubbed her stomach, and pantomimed chewing and drinking motions.

"Food?" Tracie asked.

Loren nodded, pointing to Boy 11, who continued to attack the rock and put loose pieces of stone in the ore chute, oblivious of them or anyone else.

"Oh, you mean lunch. We'll talk to him then."

Loren smiled.

With a sigh, Tracie hit the wall hard with her hammer. It was just early morning and they had to work here till these zombie miners stopped for their lunch break. *Damn!*

The unexpected loud clanging of a bell overpowered the drilling and pounding noises in the bowels of the mine. Within seconds, all the workers surrounding Loren and Tracie dropped their tools into the large bin and dashed into the hallway, most heading left toward the elevator area.

Tracie glanced at her watch. "It's noon," she whispered in the now eerily quiet surroundings. "Lunchtime, I guess."

"Let's follow them," Loren said. "But after drinking all that water, I gotta pee. Wonder where these people go to the bathroom here."

The girls hurried to catch up with the miners and followed the group as they continued along the corridor. Tracie tapped Loren's shoulder and pointed to a man as he grabbed a small mine car parked on the side of the hall and opened the lid on the top. Then, with his back to them, he unzipped his pants and proceeded to urinate.

Both girls looked away as they listened to the recognizable tinkling sound. "Must be some kind of mine porta-potty," Loren whispered.

"I hope there's a more private one for the women," Tracie murmured.

"We're supposed to be men, remember?" Loren pointed to her facial hair.

"Oh yeah. I guess I'm getting used to the dumb beard 'cause I forgot about it. Anyway, there're no women around us here. Let's keep walking and see if we can find something we can use."

Several yards ahead, the girls found another toilet car and took turns using it. By the time they reached the corner lunch table, the miners were already eating their midday meals. Some sat on benches next to the table, but most of the men lined the sides of the hallway, sitting on the damp ground and leaning against the rock wall.

Loren and Tracie retrieved their lunch boxes from the corner where they had shoved them, returned to the corridor, sat, and examined their food.

"I'm good," Tracie whispered, unwrapping her peanut butter and jelly sandwich.

"Just make sure it's our water," Loren said softly, pointing to the miners who all drank similar-looking unlabeled bottles of clear liquid. "We don't want to make a mistake and drink theirs."

Tracie lifted her bottle and smiled. A small red star was taped to the bottom.

Raising her water, Loren found the same red star and nodded. "Eat fast," she whispered. "We've gotta find Boy 11 before they all go back."

The girls finished their meals, tossed the lunchboxes into the same corner, and again each took a bottle of water. Then they started walking slowly, surveying the hallway.

Some of the miners had risen from the floor or bench, having finished their noon meals. The girls heard the noises of toilet cars being used, but the only other sounds were an occasional cough or grunt, and some short phrases—"I am next" or "Thank you." There were no conversations.

After searching for several minutes, Tracie tugged Loren's hand and pointed to a young miner sitting by himself and gazing straight ahead at the empty corridor.

"Hello," Loren said, crouching next to the blond-haired boy. "You must be new here." She tried to lower her voice and speak in a monotone. "What is your name?"

"I am Man 4." The boy's blank expression didn't change.

"Do you know Boy 11?" Loren continued. "I must find him."

"No. My name is Man 4."

"You do not know where Boy 11 is?" Loren repeated. "It is important that I find him."

"No. I do not know Boy..."

The bell clanged again, this time creating a deafening noise in the surrounding silence, and the boy and all the other miners immediately returned to their workstations.

Tracie glanced at Loren and sadly shook her head. "He's a robot like all the others," she shouted, again having to compete with the cacophony of drilling and hammering noises. "What are we gonna do now?"

"We're gonna get out of here. There's nothing else we can learn by spending the afternoon standing in this hot dark cave and hammering a rock wall." Loren looked at her fingers. "I think I'm already getting blisters."

The two girls retraced their paths through the now deserted hallway back to the area by the corner table where the miners had eaten lunch. "Should we take our lunchboxes?" Tracie asked.

"Yeah, just in case someone with a working brain comes down to check later and sees them still here." She and Tracie picked up their pails and continued toward the elevator, which rested at the bottom of the shaft.

"I don't know how this thing works," Loren said, opening the door of the slatted cage. "Must be a button to press somewhere."

"I don't care how it works. I'm not riding in this creepy old elevator again." Tracie backed away. "And what if it's not supposed to go up again until the miners are done working? There's gotta be another way to get to the top."

"Yeah." Loren nodded as she closed the elevator door. "Old mines like this usually have ramps so let's look around. I thought I saw an opening in the hall."

Again the two girls entered the corridor, stopping every few feet to shine their headlamps along both sides. As they reached the work area, it grew noisier. Two heavily muscled men were moving a mine car filled with stone from the end of the ore chute and replacing it with an empty car while the other miners attacked the wall. None of them turned to look at Tracie and Loren, who snapped a few more photos.

"Here!" Tracie grabbed Loren's arm and pointed to an area on the left that jutted out from the hallway. The pair rushed to the opening and beamed their headlamps at it.

"You were right," Tracie said. "This is a ramp, with tracks, going up. Pretty steep, I think."

"Want to give it a try? It may not go all the way to the top."

"Anything but that elevator!" Tracie pointed her light at the incline, stepped onto the ramp, and started walking.

The girls worked their way along the ramp, often holding on to the rock wall for balance and trying not to slip on the tracks. The upward climb was eerily quiet, with only the fading sounds of drills.

"I hope this leads us out," Tracie whispered. "I sure don't want to have to go all the way back down to the bottom."

"And take the elevator."

"Yeah."

As they walked, the girls passed three other levels of the mine, but all seemed deserted. Finally, the ramp ended and they stood in the middle of a dark hallway.

"Okay," Tracie said softly. "Which way do you want to go?"

"Out, wherever that is. But let's stop here first." Loren lowered her body onto the rock ground. "My legs are killing me."

Tracie sat next to her. "We can rest later, but right now, we should get the hell out of here in case someone comes." She beamed her headlamp in each direction. "Both sides look empty and I don't hear anything. Pick one."

"Let's try this way." Loren shone her light toward the left and the girls continued their trek.

What's that noise? Lance Kimbrough, standing in the top level of the mine, immediately stopped his examination of the wall and listened intently. With all the workers stationed at the bottom of the shaft, it had been totally silent. But now, suddenly, he heard a series of soft shuffling noises. *Footsteps?* Anxiously, the geologist picked up his notebook and rushed toward the sounds.

After shining his headlamp in the vicinity of the noises, he caught a glimpse of a pair of blue jumpsuits just before they disappeared from his view. They seemed to be heading toward the mine's exit.

"Stop!" he shouted. "Where are you two going? Today's work's not done yet! You can't just leave!"

Kimbrough ran to the opening that led out of the mine and stepped into the hot summer afternoon. He rotated his head back and forth, but didn't see anyone.

He stood there, totally perplexed, wondering what had just happened. His workers never left before the evening bell without his permission. And none of them had ever just walked out of the mine. They always listened to everything he said—and he had ordered those two to stop. *What was going on?*

As he wandered around the exterior of the mine looking for the disobedient miners, Kimbrough considered the best way to handle this disturbing situation. First he'd have to do a roll call at the end of the day to determine who was missing. Then he'd have to let Dugan know and, of course, the sheriff would tell Merlynn. The geologist sighed. The mine owner wouldn't like this incident at all, not one little bit.

"Is he gone?" Tracie whispered to Loren as they hid in a thick clump of sagebrush behind the mine.

"He walked into the building over there and I don't see him anymore. But let's wait a little longer, just in case. We were lucky to get out. Another couple of seconds and he would've found us."

"That guy sounded surprised, but also hurt and confused."

"Well, yeah," Loren said. "We didn't act anything like the other miners...Do you think he doesn't know what's going on here?"

"How could he not know? All he has to do is look at those zombie people."

"I guess. But then why'd he call all their numbers first to check that they were here?"

"I don't know. Maybe he just likes to pretend he's running a normal mine operation. Everything about this place is weird."

"Yeah," Loren agreed. "Did you notice that none of the miners were our age? I mean, there was Boy 11 and the other kid, but no older teens. I wonder why."

Tracie shrugged. "Well, we know they're not in school. Maybe they're working someplace else."

"Maybe." Loren stepped out from the bush and glanced quickly in all directions. "Let's find our clothes real fast and get out of here before that guy comes back. Then we can try to figure out our next step. We gotta save Boy 11 and the rest of them."

"I can't wait to get this stupid thing off my face," Tracie said as Loren drove the Jeep back to their motel. "I'm afraid to pull it off."

Without being detected, the girls had grabbed their clothes, dashed to the opening in the fence, and driven away from the mine. A few miles out of Corsonia, Loren had parked the car behind some rocks and they had taken off the blue jumpsuits and put on their jeans and tops.

"The beard?" Loren asked. "With everything that's happened today, that's what you're worried about?"

"Yeah, and getting a rash or some disease from wearing that disgusting mining suit. At least that's stuff I can do something about. I have no idea how we're gonna rescue Boy 11 and all those other zombies."

"We can't close the mine, that's for sure. Those workers aren't gonna go on strike."

"True," Tracie agreed, leaning back in the seat. "They're just gonna keep pounding that stone wall."

"Only until we figure out a way to switch them back into real people."

"I'm listening." Tracie turned toward the driver.

"I'm working on it," Loren said. "I just need a little more time."

CHAPTER 14

Early Wednesday night, Lance Kimbrough stood in Merlynn's regal office next to Sheriff Dugan, feeling like a negligent shepherd who had lost track of part of his flock. After telling his story to the sheriff, Dugan had phoned his boss, who had ordered the geologist to immediately report to her.

Kimbrough had just finished recounting the episode of the mysterious two workers rushing out of the mine. Now he waited for Merlynn's reaction, having no idea what it would be.

The woman studied him intently before she spoke. "And you're sure no one on your list was missing?" she asked.

"I checked the numbers twice at the end of the workday and every person was accounted for."

"Were you able to tell if the people you saw were men or women?" Merlynn continued.

The geologist shook his head. "I only saw the uniforms, nothing else."

"So how'd they get in?" Dugan asked.

"I don't know." Kimbrough shrugged. "It doesn't make any sense.

Why would anyone want to sneak into the mine?"

"Could be industrial spies," Merlynn said. "Another mine operation that wants to discover exactly what we're doing, maybe found out how successful we are."

"You really think so?" Kimbrough asked. "I've done as you said and kept it a secret. I never said a word to anyone."

"Whoever those two are, they're breaking the law by trespassing on my property and it's likely they're either spies or thieves or both." Merlynn turned to the sheriff. "How many of our people do you have guarding the mine?"

"Just one. We never had any problems."

She shook her head. "Well, we do now. I want armed guards posted all along the fence. At least ten, maybe even fifteen— whatever it takes to cover all the ground."

"Is that really necessary?" Kimbrough asked. "Do you think those intruders are so dangerous?"

Merlynn leaned her massive body forward and reached into the Hostess box for a cupcake. "Yes," she said, unwrapping the treat. "I certainly do."

"Just a couple of scared teenage girls, huh?" Merlynn said to Dugan. While she waited for his response, she took a big bite of her cupcake.

The geologist had been dismissed, but the sheriff still stood in front of the fat woman's desk, nervously twirling his hat in his hand and glancing at the floor. "I didn't think they'd cause this much trouble," he muttered. Then, raising his head, he met Merlynn's cold green eyes. "But if those girls are dumb enough to come back into Corsonia, they won't get away again. I'll make sure of it."

"You'd better. They already know too much."

"What about Kimbrough?"

Merlynn shook her head. "The man knows rocks, but he has no

clue about people."

"Yeah. He still doesn't get it. You think what happened today will make him suspicious?"

She laughed loudly. "Not a chance."

"Merlynn, about all the guards. You know we're gonna have to pull some workers out of the mine. It'll cut down on our production."

"It can't be helped. I want people posted everywhere—houses, schools, stores, as well as the mine."

"Yes, ma'am."

"I'll order the guards to capture any intruders." She checked her watch. "We'll do a TV broadcast in fifteen minutes. Get the camera ready."

"Certainly, Merlynn."

"Good." She waved her hand, signaling the meeting was over, and held onto the desk for support as she prepared to stand.

"Umm, I got an idea," the sheriff said, again twisting his Stetson. "Maybe tomorrow I should go look for those girls in Montello. That's the closest place to here with a motel so I figure that's gotta be where they're staying. I can do some checking up on who they are. What do you think?"

Still leaning on her desk, Merlynn nodded, her flabby chin bobbing up and down. "Not a bad thought, Tom. It could help to find out more about those two—why they're so interested in our little town. Also, it might give us a better clue on how get rid of them." With her right hand, she reached for the rest of the cupcake, tossed it into her mouth, and savored it. "Just make sure you're real careful so nobody notices what you're doing. Now I'm going to get ready for tonight's performance—Woman 3!"

On Thursday morning, Sheriff Dugan drove his black SUV into Montello and parked it near the motel. Then, strolling leisurely, he walked to the next corner, entered the Tasty Grill, and lowered his burly body onto a counter stool of the nearly empty restaurant.

Dugan wore his usual western outfit—Stetson, plaid shirt, jeans, and cowboy boots. He had purposely kept a low profile since his days as disgraced mayor of Corsonia so he wasn't well known in Montello and didn't expect to be recognized. But, just in case someone in the town had a long memory, the sheriff had added a simple disguise: black-framed eyeglasses and a short brown wig.

He picked up the laminated menu and glanced at it. "What's good this morning?" he asked the skinny blonde waitress wearing a "Brenda" nametag, who stood behind the counter.

"Everything 'cept the hash browns. Cook burnt them." The middle-aged woman smiled, revealing a mouthful of gleaming white teeth. "So what can I get for you? Coffee's real good."

"I'll take a cup." He returned her smile.

The waitress poured the coffee and Dugan took a hearty sip. "Yeah," he said, nodding his head. "You're right. This is really good." Then he scanned the restaurant. "How's business? Don't see too many folks in here."

"Yeah. We're kinda slow right now, but most of the breakfast crowd's already done. We pick up again for lunch." She flashed her toothy smile again. "So what're you gonna have?"

The sheriff took another look at the menu. "How about a ham omelet with fries? I'll take your advice and skip the hash browns."

"Good choice." After snatching his menu, the waitress continued through the swinging door to the kitchen.

When she returned, Dugan smiled at her again and resumed the conversation. "Get many strangers in here or only locals?"

"Most are people I know, but we do get some folks from out of town. Why're you asking?"

"Just curious. I don't live here so I was wondering about some of your other customers."

"Oh? Where you from?"

"Wells," Dugan said, naming a town in the middle of Elko

County, near Interstate 80. "You go there much?"

"Yeah, sometimes. They got the airport there."

"Harriet Field...So any other interesting folks besides me come in here lately?"

"Not many. But there's a couple of girls from New York, traveling across the country on their summer vacation, who've been stopping in for about a week."

"Really?" The sheriff chuckled. "Wonder what they're finding to do around these parts."

"Well, they told me they like looking at the old mines and taking pictures. Checked out Delano."

"Nothing left of that one to photograph," he said, smiling. "I've been there too. Guess they're staying at the motel."

"Probably." She shrugged. "It's the only place in town." Then she flashed her smile again. "'Cuse me. I'm gonna go back and check on your breakfast. Should be ready by now."

Sheriff Dugan sauntered out of the Tasty Grill satisfied with the snippets of information he had learned from the waitress. *Nothing to this questioning shit,* he thought smugly as he walked to his SUV.

After she had brought him his food, he hadn't asked the waitress any more probing questions about the New York girls, figuring that would have sounded too suspicious. Instead, he had chatted about the weather and what was happening locally—not much, of course. *And the omelet was damn good,* he thought, rubbing his protruding stomach.

When he reached the car, he opened the door and sat down. "Maybe I'll get lucky and they're still inside," he muttered, glancing at the small motel. He didn't want to take a chance, go in there, and have them recognize him. "Blow my cover," he mumbled, recalling the police term. Besides, he had no power in Montello.

Better to just wait here. The sheriff stretched his legs, leaned against the seat, and made himself comfortable, ready to begin his stakeout.

Late Thursday morning, Loren and Tracie were on the last leg of a quick road tour of Corsonia.

"That's too bad," Loren muttered as she drove the Jeep away from the boys' school before the armed guard noticed them.

"Well, what did you expect after that guy saw us in the mine yesterday?" Tracie asked.

"He didn't get a clear look, especially with our men's disguise so he couldn't have known we're girls."

"But he saw people running out of the mine because he yelled for us to stop."

"Yeah. He did."

"Anyway, if he tells the sheriff, they'll figure it was us," Tracie pointed out. "Nobody else has been snooping around here."

"Okay. So they've got zombie people with rifles everywhere we've been today—at the shopping center, at the boys' house and school, and probably at all their other places. But it wasn't a complete waste of time. We did see a man in that old rusty truck picking up the bottles of water at the store around ten so we know he's gotta be delivering them to the people. Too bad we couldn't follow him to find out where he went."

"Right!" Tracie snorted. "Those two guards with rifles would've loved that. Lucky they didn't see us and shoot."

"Of course, we didn't check the mine," Loren continued. "But we can't go back there."

"Finally, you're making sense. They've gotta be guarding the mine. That's what they're trying so hard to hide."

"True," Loren said. "So there's nothing we can do here to save Boy 11, Boy 12, and everyone else. Let's go back to Montello and finish working on our rescue plan."

Tracie sighed deeply. "It's a good plan—but only if we can

carry it out without getting caught." She shook her head. "If we're captured, those robot people won't listen to anything we say about helping them. They'll either kill us on the spot or bring us to their boss, who'll turn us into zombies."

"Yeah," Loren agreed. "Not the greatest choices."

Sheriff Dugan reclined in his car, watching the Montello traffic, if you could call it that. Every five minutes or so, a car or a truck passed by—and this was the town's main street. *Sure won't miss nothing.*

When he heard the sound of an approaching vehicle, he raised his head, and followed a green Jeep as it pulled into the motel's small lot. Then two girls, a blonde and a shorter brunette, stepped out and entered the building.

"Damn," he muttered. "They switched cars." The teens were cleverer than he had figured, not just a couple of silly party girls, and they were still hanging around here so they must be planning something. *But what?* Without asking too many suspicious questions, he had to think of a way to learn more.

He leaned back in his seat and closed his eyes, trying to figure out a good next move.

"Let's get going," Loren said.

"Okay, just give me a second." Tracie finished twisting a rubber band around her ponytail. "Want to grab some lunch before we get started?" she asked.

"Sure, as long as it's fast."

The girls dashed out of the motel and walked toward the Tasty Grill, neither of them noticing the black SUV parked across the street. They entered the restaurant and sat in a front booth.

The thin blonde waitress placed two menus on the table and

smiled at them. "Nice seeing you girls again," she said, showing off her sparkling teeth. "Funny 'cause I was just talking about you."

"Oh really, Brenda." Tracie lowered her menu and glanced at the woman.

"Yeah. A man came in 'bout an hour ago and asked me if any strangers had stopped in here lately. I told him about you two girls being from New York."

"What did he look like?" Loren asked, trying to keep her voice calm.

"Short heavy guy with glasses and brown hair. Wore a Stetson." She turned her head from Loren to Tracie. "You two know him?"

"Not really," Tracie said. "But we may have met him once." She smiled sweetly at the waitress. "Can you do us a favor and, if he comes in here again and asks any more questions, just don't tell him about this conversation—or anything else—and leave a message for us at the motel?"

"Sure. Hey, I'm sorry if I did anything wrong." The woman's smile faded and her expression registered a look of concern. "You girls in some kind of trouble that I can help you with?"

"No," Loren said. "Right now, we're fine. And you didn't do anything wrong, Brenda. But thanks for the offer because we'll need your help if that man comes back."

"Sure," the waitress said, smiling once again. "I'll be glad to help."

Sheriff Dugan waited until the girls were inside the restaurant. Then he sprinted from the car and darted into the lobby of the motel. "Afternoon," he said, nodding to the elderly woman behind the desk.

"Howdy. Need a room today?"

"Not today, thanks. Got a favor to ask though. I want to surprise a couple of young ladies from out of town that've been staying here with you."

"Oh?" the clerk looked confused. "The girls didn't tell me they knew anyone from around here."

"We met a few days ago back in Wells and I promised to visit and say hello when I came into Montello so I'd like to knock on their door and tell them I'm here. I just need their room number." Dugan shrugged, trying to look casual.

"The girls are out right now. I saw them leave a little while ago so you just missed them. Sorry."

"Did they say when they're coming back? I'm going home soon and was hoping to see them."

"No. They're usually out for most of the day. Must be doing lots of sightseeing, I guess. They like taking pictures of old mines. Showed me some."

"Can I slip a note under their door then?"

"It's easier for me to give it to them." She smiled at the sheriff. "We don't give out room numbers unless our guests tell us to. Safety reasons."

"I understand," Dugan said, trying to hide his disappointment. "You got a piece of paper and an envelope I can use?"

"Sure." The clerk tore off a page from a pad and handed it to him along with an envelope.

Dugan used the pen on the counter to write a short note, which he folded, put inside the envelope, and sealed. "Thanks," he said.

"No problem. I'll make sure the girls get your letter."

"You think it's the sheriff who's asking questions?" Tracie said when the waitress left. "He's the only one besides the zombies who wants us out of here."

"Yeah, probably, although he wasn't wearing glasses and didn't have much hair when we met him."

"Could be a disguise—and if it's not him, then it's someone else from Corsonia that's been sent by their boss to find us." Tracie turned to her friend. "So now that they know where we are, what're we gonna do?"

"Continue with our plan." Loren nodded her head. "They always had to know we were staying here. Montello's the nearest town and this is the only motel."

"But why come here now and start checking up on us?"

"I don't know. But it means we gotta be real careful in Montello too and watch everybody and everything."

Tracie sighed. "I thought we could at least relax when we were here. This was supposed to be our fun vacation, remember?"

"I know and I'm really sorry, Trace. But think about those poor zombies trapped in the mine and those boys in the school." Loren shook her head sadly. "They don't have any kind of life, never mind a vacation. Boy 11's already a robot and Boy 12's supposed to 'graduate' school tomorrow. We gotta finish loading up our supplies and start working on saving all of them."

After lunch, Loren and Tracie left the Tasty Grill and headed back to the motel to get the Jeep. This time, they checked the street as they walked, but since the sheriff's black SUV was no longer parked nearby, they didn't see anything suspicious.

They spent the rest of the afternoon shopping in several of the town's stores before returning to the Montello Inn. In the motel's parking lot, Loren took out a gray tarp they had bought. "Just in case someone walks by and thinks all this is a little strange," she said as she and Tracie covered their purchases with the tarp. Then the girls went to their room to get ready for dinner.

Tracie unlocked the door and immediately noticed the envelope on the floor. She picked it up, opened it, and glanced at the paper inside.

"Read it out loud," Loren said.

"It's written in all capital letters and it says: 'I KNOW WHERE YOU GIRLS ARE. LEAVE WHILE YOU STILL CAN. YOU DONT

BELONG HERE AND THIS IS NOT YOUR BUSINESS. GET OUT BEFORE ITS TO LATE.'" Tracie looked up. "It's signed, 'A FRIEND.'"

"Some friend," Loren said, jumping on the bed. "I guess this is supposed to scare us."

"Yeah—and it's working. I'm scared."

"This whole thing is scary, Trace, I know. But this guy can't do anything to us, at least not here."

"He and the rest of them can do plenty to us in Corsonia though. Shouldn't we tell the police?"

Loren shrugged. "What're they gonna do? This note doesn't even sound that bad unless you understand what's going on in that weird place. And we already know that the people here don't want anything to do with the 'Hippy Town.'"

"But if we tell them about the mine, the boys..."

"We have no proof so they'll just think we're nuts."

"What about all the pictures you've been taking, Lor?"

"There's nothing that connects those photos to Corsonia either. And even if we could somehow convince the police to investigate, how many officers do you think they'd send? One? Two? Then whose fault would it be if they got caught—or worse—killed? We need an army and they're not gonna send that."

Loren shook her head before continuing. "The problem is we still don't know who's in charge. We've gotta do this by ourselves so let's go on with our plan and just hope the sheriff and the zombies don't catch us."

CHAPTER 15

Friday morning, at the break of dawn, Loren drove toward the abandoned shopping center in Corsonia. "Are you good with the plan?" she asked Tracie.

"Yeah, except for the stuff about what we have to do if anything goes wrong," her friend mumbled.

"It's important. This is the only way we can save these people so we have to take a chance." Loren shook her head. "I don't think we have any choice."

"I just hope it works." Tracie patted her long, dark brown beard. "I thought that the goatee was a pain, but this thing is even worse. I can't believe you had it on for the whole day."

"We gotta do it. I don't want those guards to figure out who we are and, with their brains not working, maybe they'll just remember the beards and hats." Both girls wore ponytails under black Stetsons. Loren took a quick glance at her hirsute friend and smiled. "You do look like a mean bad guy."

"But I don't know if I can act like one, Lor, especially since the zombies aren't really bad people."

"Well, just remember that they've been told to hurt, maybe even kill us, so we've gotta deal with them."

Tracie leaned back in the seat and sighed. "I just want all this to be over."

"It will be, very soon."

Loren swerved off the road before Corsonia's shopping center and parked the Jeep behind several large bushes. "Okay," she said, smiling at Tracie. "Here we go...Ready?"

"I guess."

The two girls walked silently to the far right of the deserted business area, continuing past the backs of the empty line of stores, toward the last building. When they reached Phil's Food Mart, Loren tapped Tracie's shoulder and pointed to the bearded and ponytailed young man who stood in front of the rear door, holding his rifle loosely in his arms.

"Now," Loren whispered. Both girls ran at the man and knocked him to the ground before he had a chance to raise the weapon and fire a shot.

"Hold him!" Loren ordered as she sat on the man's stomach, clamped her left hand over his mouth, and, with her other hand, took a syringe from her pants pocket. As Tracie clutched the man's arms, Loren injected the stunned guard and waited several seconds until he closed his eyes.

"So far, so good," Loren whispered, standing and tossing the empty syringe into the shrubs. "Lemme check if he's got a key to the store." She reached inside his shirt and pants pockets. "Nothing— not even a wallet."

"Then the other guy better have the key. We don't want to have to break in and let them know something's wrong here."

"Yeah." Loren faced Tracie. "Let's tie this guy up in case he wakes up before we're done."

"He should be out for at least two hours."

"You're not an expert on knockout drugs," Loren whispered.

"I got an A in chemistry and checked this formula online. It'll work."

"We're still using the rope."

"Fine."

Tracie handed her friend the cord she carried in her jeans and Loren tied the man's arms together and then bound his legs. Next Loren took a roll of cellophane tape from her shirt pocket, tore off a piece, and taped his mouth. "If he's still asleep when we're done, we'll cut him loose," she whispered. "Okay. One down, one more to go."

The two girls walked to the far corner of the food store and, slowly and silently, inched their way toward the front. When they reached the corner, Loren held up her hand, signaling Tracie to stop. Then she stuck out her head and took a quick peek. Another bearded longhaired man, this one taller and heftier than the first guard, stood facing the other direction, holding a rifle.

Loren pointed toward the front of the store and mimicked a person firing a rifle.

Tracie nodded.

"Now," Loren whispered and both girls rushed at the guard.

The man turned around just as Loren and Tracie landed on top of him. All three of them tumbled heavily to the ground, the rifle rolling several feet away.

"Got him?" Loren asked as she tried to hold the stunned man down with her left hand.

"No!" Tracie shouted. "He's too strong."

The bearded man threw Tracie off his stomach and she fell hard on her elbow.

"Oww!"

"Trace!" Loren yelled. "I need you to hold him down!"

"Easy for you to say!"

The bearded man sat up and reached for his rifle.

"No!" Tracie shouted again as she dove headfirst at the guard's body, landing on his massive chest. "Hurry!" she urged.

Loren shoved another filled syringe into the guard's arm.

"What...are...you...doing?" the man asked, finally speaking as he struggled to break free of the girls' grasp. "Who...are...?" He closed his eyes before he was able to finish the second question.

"He didn't even scream," Tracie said, handing her friend the cord. "I guess these zombie people don't have any emotions either. But that guy's super strong. My elbow really hurts." She massaged the aching limb.

"Sorry, Trace. I'm just glad the drug kicked in before he was able to get loose. Now I'm gonna tie up this one really tight and then let's drag him next to the other one."

After they relocated the guard and removed the key from his shirt pocket, Loren unlocked the rear door of Phil's Food Mart. Then she drove the Jeep to the back entrance and the girls started their transfer. Using a newly-purchased dolly, they wheeled in the two hundred and fifty bottles of water they had bought during their shopping trip to several stores in Montello—not wanting to arouse suspicion by buying too many cases in one place. In the evening, they had gone back to the Jeep and painstakingly removed all the labels so that their bottles now looked identical to the water supply housed in the store.

Working as quickly as they could, Loren and Tracie exchanged each of the cartons of water bottles on the floor, being careful not to confuse the new bottles with the others.

"Okay, that's the last one," Tracie said when the final bottle had been switched, the tainted water spilled out, and the empty bottles hidden under the gray tarp. "We've got about twenty extra of our water. Think we should leave them, Lor?"

"Yeah. I bet they don't count the bottles too carefully. They probably just use all the water they have here."

The girls left the remaining bottles in a partially filled carton on the floor.

"Let's check on the guards, return the key, and then get out of here before someone comes," Tracie said as she stood up.

"Good idea."

The girls rushed to the side near the back of the store where they had left the guards.

"See, I told you my formula would work," Tracie said, staring at the two unconscious men.

"I hope you didn't kill them," Loren said as she returned the key to the beefy guard's shirt pocket.

Tracie removed the tape from the mouth of one of the men and stuck her hand under his nose. "He's still breathing," she said. "They'll both be fine in another hour or so." She lifted the man's roped hands toward Loren. "Use your knife to cut the cord."

Sheriff Dugan usually began his daily patrol of Corsonia at the shopping center. Since it was empty except for the water warehouse, he liked to get there early and then check the boys' and girls' schools and the various houses. Other than making the necessary pickups and deliveries, he avoided visiting the mine, preferring not to deal with Lance Kimbrough, whom he privately referred to as "that idiot scientist." The man knew everything about gold, but otherwise was a hopeless moron. Besides, Dugan had plenty of guards posted at the mine and didn't think the girls would return so soon.

What're they up to? he wondered as he continued toward the deserted stores. Two teenage girls from New York should have better things to do than stick their noses into his business. *How much do they know?* They had been snooping around the boys' school and talked to one of them, but the kid didn't know anything, and now he'd been taken care of.

Dugan drove his black SUV into the center and slowed down as he glanced at each of the abandoned stores.

As she watched Loren finish cutting the cord binding the second guard's feet, Tracie tucked the coil of rope into her pocket and quickly raised her head. "Is that a car?" she asked.

"I think so. Move it!"

The girls ran toward the Jeep, reaching the vehicle just as Dugan's SUV pulled into the rear of the food mart.

The sheriff jumped out of the car and aimed his gun at them. "Stop or I'll shoot!" he yelled.

Tracie opened the passenger's door while Loren dashed to the driver's side.

The pinging sounds of gunshots filled the air and Loren fell to the ground, her hands grasping the bottom of the door. "Oww!" she cried. "He shot me in the leg!"

"I'll pull you up." Tracie crawled into the driver's seat and opened the door as bullet noises again echoed around them.

"No! I can't move, and if you don't get out of here fast, he'll just kill us both and ruin everything. Go now—follow the plan." Loren tossed her car keys, wallet, and phone on the seat, slammed the door shut, and pushed her body away from the car. "Get the hell out of here!" she shouted as a bullet hit the rear window, shattering the glass.

Tracie picked up Loren's keys, turned on the ignition and, as the sheriff pointed his gun at her, ducked, pressed down hard on the gas pedal, and sped away from Corsonia.

"Damn!" Dugan muttered, watching the Jeep disappear from his view. "Well, at least I got one of them." Still holding his loaded gun in front of him, he headed toward the wounded girl.

Loren remained in a sitting position, dragging her bleeding left leg toward the store in an attempt to distance herself from the approaching man. However, moving was painful, and, realizing escape was impossible, she stopped and waited for him to reach her.

"Not as smart as you thought, huh, missy—or should I call you mister with that dumb beard?" Dugan smirked as he aimed his gun at Loren. "Oughta just kill you for all the trouble you've made, but I got orders to bring you back..."

"To your boss, right?"

"Pretty nosy, ain't you now?"

"Just curious about who's doing all of this."

"What do you mean 'all of this'?"

"The mine. Who owns it?"

Sheriff Dugan nodded his head. "So that *was* you in the mine. How'd you two get in there?"

Loren shrugged.

"Don't matter much now, anyway." He looked at the sleeping guards. "What'd you do to them?"

"Just knocked them out for a while. They'll be okay in an hour or so."

"What were you doing here, anyway?"

"Just looking around, trying to figure out what was going on."

"Oh." He stared at her. "And what did you find?"

Loren shrugged again. "Nothing much—just a lot of water in there."

Still pointing his gun at her, the sheriff backed away and twisted the doorknob of the storeroom. It was locked. "Yeah," he said, glancing inside and noticing the bottles were filled and in their cases. "You'll be drinking some of that real soon."

Loren didn't respond.

"It's a special kind of water," he continued. "Very tasty." Then, returning to the SUV, Dugan removed a pair of handcuffs from the glove compartment and secured Loren's wrists. "Now I'm gonna get you into my car." He glared at her. "And if you try anything stupid, I'm gonna shoot you in the other leg."

Tracie drove quickly toward the county road, looking over her shoulder every few seconds to make sure she wasn't being followed, not that she expected to be tailed since the sheriff was busy with Loren and he seemed to work alone.

Tears streamed down her face as she thought of her injured friend. *How could I just leave her?* If they were right about what was happening, Loren would be turned into one of them—another mindless zombie.

She shook her head and wiped away the flowing tears. *But if I stayed?* What good would that have done? Then they'd both be robots, with no one to save them. Loren and all those poor people of Corsonia were counting on her. *It's up to me now. Be brave like Loren.*

Tracie remembered an incident not long after they had met in middle school. She'd been walking to the mall with Loren when a small dog, a stick in its mouth, dashed into the middle of the road.

Without saying a word, Loren immediately ran into the street and scooped up the gray and white dog—just before a car screeched to a stop two feet from hitting her. When Loren was safely back on the sidewalk, Tracie's heart had continued to pound from the scare.

"Why did you do that?" she had asked. "You could've been killed."

"But I wasn't, was I? And I saved the dog."

That was Loren—brave and impulsive. *A dangerous combination.* But, right now, Tracie needed some of her friend's strength. *Be brave like Loren.*

She turned onto CR-766 and headed toward Montello, trying to forget about Loren's plight and focus on what she had to do. It was time for the next phase of their plan.

CHAPTER 16

Merlynn leaned her elbows on the desk and cupped her hands around her jowly cheeks as she smiled at the handcuffed blonde teen sitting in front of her. "So what were you and your friend doing at the stores so early this morning?" she asked. "And why'd you drug the guards?"

Loren didn't respond. The fat lady had ordered one of her servants—a young girl zombie—to clean and bandage her wound, but the leg still throbbed.

"Where's your friend?"

Loren looked at the green-eyed woman, but said nothing.

"She just left you and drove away, even though you were hurt? Some friend." Merlynn nodded, still smiling sweetly. "You know, the two of you have caused me a lot of trouble—and I don't like trouble. That disguise, for instance." She pointed to the girl's beard. "Is that what you wore when you trespassed and entered my mine on Wednesday?"

Loren studied the square white tiles on the office floor and didn't respond.

"What about that boy you and your friend talked to? What did he tell you?"

The girl continued to examine the ground.

"So you're not going to answer any questions—not even tell me your name?"

Dugan, who had been leaning against the wall near the desk and holding his hat, spoke for the first time. "Give her to me and I'll make her answer everything."

Merlynn waved her hand dismissively. "That won't be necessary, Tom. It doesn't really matter what she knows—since you got there before they did anything—and I don't want you to damage her." She smiled. "This one's too pretty to destroy and she won't be a problem after tonight anyway."

"What about her dark-haired friend?" the sheriff asked.

"You're going to Montello to get her and bring her back. In fact, you may as well do that right now since I don't need you here anymore. I can take care of this one all by myself."

"Okay, Merlynn. "Dugan put on his Stetson and dashed out of the office.

Using her elbows for support, the obese woman pushed herself out of her chair and waddled over to Loren, this time, scowling at the girl. Then, with a quick thrust of her hand, she yanked off the fake beard.

"Owww!" Loren shrieked, her eyes welling with tears.

"Sorry, dear," Merlynn said, again smiling. "But that's enough of the hairy look. You're so much prettier without it—and I really do like pretty blonde girls." She turned away from Loren and raised her voice. "Man 24! Come in here!"

Within seconds, the tall lanky servant limped into the office and gazed at Merlynn with vacant eyes.

"Take her to the laboratory and put her in the chair."

The man immediately grabbed the girl by her handcuffs, pulled her roughly through the doorway, and dragged her along the lengthy corridor and up the steps. When he reached the laboratory, he threw Loren inside and she landed heavily on the hard tiled floor. "Ow!" she cried, grasping her injured leg.

"Why are you here?" a timid voice asked.

As Man 24 picked her up, Loren caught a quick glimpse of a boy with cropped black hair strapped into one of two reclining chairs in the center of the room. "Boy 12, is that you?"

"Yes."

"That's right. Today is Friday. Tonight's the full moon."

"What will happen to me? I am very frightened."

"It will be okay, Boy 12," Loren said, smiling at him despite her pain as the man pushed her into the second chair. "When the fat woman comes in here, try not to pay too much attention to her because she's just going to want to upset you."

"Will she hurt me?"

Loren shook her head. "I don't think so. She'll talk to you, maybe say some bad things, and make you drink some water." She forced herself to keep smiling at the boy. "It'll all be okay. We're both gonna fall asleep and afterwards, when we wake up, things will be better."

That last part was a lie, of course, but she didn't want to scare the boy even more. And, if the plan worked, things would be better. *But not right away.* That was the big problem.

About five minutes later, Loren and Boy 12 heard heavy footsteps approaching and Merlynn entered the room. "So I see you two have met," she said, smiling. "How very nice to make new friends."

"Please do not hurt me," Boy 12 pleaded. "Let me return to the school. I will be better and learn more."

Merlynn shook her head. "Sorry, kid, but I'm afraid that's not gonna happen. I need new workers and you're old enough to do the job so it's graduation time." Smiling again, she waddled to a counter that contained several bottles filled with clear liquid and grabbed one. Then she returned to the boy and hoisted the bottle. "Congratulations! Now you're gonna drink this water to celebrate your gradu..."

"Why don't you leave him alone and let him go back?" Loren interrupted. "He's just a boy and you've got me. I'll do the work you need."

Merlynn turned toward the girl and grinned at her. "How very noble of you, dear. So that's how you picture yourself, as the brave heroine who rushes in to save the kid—sacrifice yourself for him. Joan of Arc, maybe?" She chuckled. "I think you've seen too many movies. First of all, I do need the boy and, second of all, I already have both of you and intend to keep it that way." She wagged her plump finger at Loren. "You had a chance to leave. You should have gone when the sheriff warned you, but you didn't and now you will never leave—Man 24!"

The servant, who had remained standing at attention in the rear of the laboratory, limped as quickly as he could to Merlynn's side.

"You make sure the kid's mouth stays open so I can pour in the water."

"No," the boy whimpered. "Please..."

"If you fight me, I'll have to make him hurt you and you'll drink it anyway." She smiled. "Listen, kid, it's just water. You'll feel very sleepy and then you'll have a nice long rest."

"I do not want to sleep."

"That's too bad," Merlynn said. "Now shut up and open your mouth."

Sheriff Dugan sat in his black SUV, which was parked opposite the Montello Inn, and watched the motel's front door. As soon as he had arrived in town, he'd driven past the lot and noticed the girls' green Jeep was in there, the rear window missing most of its glass, courtesy of his bullet. "Should've just killed her at the store," he muttered as he sipped the ice coffee he had just bought at the Tasty Grill. "Lousy aim. Need more practice."

He leaned against the seat and tried to get comfortable as he continued to monitor the entrance of the motel. Even if the girl used a rear door, he wouldn't miss her since the building had a tall wire fence in the back and just one access to the street. *Nothing else to do.* He didn't want to go inside and ask the clerk about the pair again. It would arouse too much suspicion, especially if the dark-haired one suddenly disappeared.

Just gotta wait. It was still morning and the girl had to come out of there sometime—if only to eat. And she'd probably return to Corsonia to try to rescue her friend. *Just gotta be patient.* She couldn't stay in the motel forever. Dugan took another sip of his drink, keeping his eyes focused on the entrance of the Montello Inn.

Loren heard soft snores in the chair next to her as Boy 12 finished drinking the tainted water and drifted into a deep sleep.

"Your turn now," Merlynn said cheerfully, holding a full bottle of water and lifting it. "I really hope you're a smart girl and won't make me force this down your throat. What do you say?"

"I'll drink it. But what're you gonna do to me after?"

The woman chuckled, her jowls bouncing. "Like I told the kid, you'll have a nice long sleep—very peaceful." She turned toward Boy 12. "See how content he is? And when you wake up, your mind will be free of all your problems. You won't care about any of this."

"How are you gonna do that?" Loren tried to remain calm and continue to ask questions, hoping the woman would reveal some information that would help when she got her mind back—*if* she got her mind back. Otherwise, of course, none of this would matter.

Merlynn stroked the girl's arm tenderly. "Sweetie, you don't have to worry about any of the complicated details. All you have to know is that things will be a lot simpler for you in a little while." Her mouth formed a wide grin. "And I'm really looking forward to having you around. You're such a pretty girl."

Loren flinched as the woman continued to caress her arm.

"Oh, you don't like that? You find me repulsive? No problem, dear." Merlynn removed her hand, smiling and nodding her head several times. "You will enjoy my affection very soon; in fact, you'll be thrilled to be with me." Her smile vanished and her expression became somber. "But that's more than enough talk. We're wasting precious time. Right now, we need to get started so your nice new life can begin and this is the first step: Have a sip of water. I hear it's quite delicious." She pressed the bottle against the girl's lips. "Drink," she ordered.

Tracie sat in the kitchen of Brenda Hartwig's Montello apartment, trying to concentrate on preparing for the next phase of the plan. But it was difficult because she kept thinking about Loren. *Should've saved her. Maybe run him down with the Jeep.* She sighed. It was much too late for "what ifs."

"You okay, hon?" Brenda asked as she popped into the room, dressed in her waitress uniform.

"Yes. I'm fine. Thank you so much for letting me stay here."

"No problem. Are you sure you don't want me to go with you tomorrow? I can get off work."

Tracie shook her head. "I need you to be here in case I don't come back. You know what to do if that happens, right?"

"Yeah. I got all the info. But I don't see why you won't call the police about your friend. I mean, you saw this sheriff guy shoot her in the leg."

"Yes. But I don't know where he took Loren and this is about a lot more than her."

"But the cops could pick the man up for questioning, especially since you figure he's here now, looking for you."

"And if he doesn't talk, what happens then? It's just my word against his and he's a sheriff. He'll just tell the police I'm crazy and making up stories. I have no proof of anything—we threw out that note in the door I told you about—so they'll have to let him go. I can't be stuck fighting a losing argument with the police when I can be working to save Loren and all the others."

"What about the broken car window?"

"I don't have any bullets to even prove the window was shot. A rock could've shattered it. Anyway, from what I've heard from people in Montello, no one wants to have anything to do with Corsonia. That's true, right?"

"Well, yeah. Folks here are afraid of that creepy town."

"And now you know why."

"That water in all those bottles you emptied, can it really turn people into zombies?"

"Yes. That's why those people there act so weird. Someone's doing this and I'm gonna find out who it is."

Merlynn finished pouring water into Loren's mouth and watched the girl's eyes close, some of the liquid trickling down her chin as she fell into a deep sleep. "Sweet dreams," the woman murmured, wiping Loren's mouth with a tissue. Then she caressed the sleeping girl's arms and traced her fat fingers lightly along the contours of Loren's face, around her chin—still red from where the beard had been attached—and over her softly pulsating chest. "You're all mine now."

Merlynn eyed the handcuffs and shook her head. "We don't need these on you anymore, dear. When you wake up, you're not going to run away." After taking a key from her pocket, she unlocked the cuffs, patted Loren's wrists, and carefully tucked the girl's arms inside the edge of the chair. "I want you to feel very comfy, sweetie. Nighty night."

Then, leaning over, she kissed Loren softly on the lips and moved a strand of blonde hair out of her eyes. "I'll let you have a good long rest now and, in a few hours, we'll have a nice little visit together. You've got a few very important things to learn." She smiled, once again caressing the girl's arm. "We're going to have so much fun together, you and me."

Mid-Friday morning, Man 33 drove the old blue pickup truck into the deserted Corsonia shopping center and parked next to the rear entrance of Phil's Food Mart. As the handsome bearded and ponytailed man removed a dolly from the truck, one of the two guards lowered his rifle and unlocked the back door. Neither man said a word.

The guard picked up his rifle and resumed his position facing away from the store while Man 33, moving quickly and methodically, began piling cartons filled with plastic bottles of water onto the dolly, which he wheeled and loaded into the truck.

The man worked by himself, without pausing and without talking to the nearby guard. There were no sounds except for the squeaking noise made by one of the wheels of his dolly. Man 33 didn't grunt, whistle, complain, or change his expression. If the cartons were heavy and he was exhausted or bored, no one would have known since his good-looking face revealed no emotion.

When he had finished loading all the bottles, Man 33 finally spoke. "Lock the store," he said in a deep monotone. "I am done." Without waiting for a response, he stepped into the truck and drove out of the shopping center to begin the second phase of his job—delivering the water to the men and women of Corsonia.

Sheriff Dugan glanced at his watch. It was nearly five o'clock. *Shit! Where the hell was she?* He'd been sitting in his car all afternoon, watching the entrance of the motel, and the girl had never come out. Except for a quick piss, his eyes had been glued to the building. He hadn't had anything to eat or drink except for the ice coffee. His stomach wasn't used to such deprivation and it was growling loudly, demanding to be fed.

He took another peek at the parking lot just to be sure and the green Jeep with the busted window was still there. *Unless...* Suddenly, he had a disturbing thought. *What if she'd used the other car—the silver one?* He'd forgotten about that.

Damn! Punching the steering wheel, Dugan shook his head in disgust. If she was driving another car, then maybe she wasn't even in the motel and that meant he'd wasted the entire afternoon sitting here. *Another half hour.* After that, he'd give up, call it a day, and go get something to eat.

He shrugged as he pondered the situation. *Not so bad.* Even if he didn't get the girl here, he was sure she'd go back to Corsonia to try to rescue her friend. He smirked at the thought. *Her friend, yeah, right. Not anymore.* He'd get the girl then. *No problem.*

CHAPTER 17

In the middle of the night early Saturday, Merlynn returned to her laboratory. With the full moon illuminating the floor to ceiling windows, she could clearly see the young boy and teenage girl, both sleeping soundly in their chairs at opposite ends of the room, where Man 24 had positioned them.

She pulled her swivel chair next to the boy and lowered her body into the seat. "Listen to me," she began, speaking softly. "I am Merlynn and I am your leader. Whenever you hear my voice, you will stop what you are doing and immediately do what I say. Do you understand?"

"Yes," Boy 12 said, his eyes still closed.

"Your name is no longer Boy 12. Your name is now Man 44 and you will answer only to that name—Man 44. Do you understand me?"

"Yes."

"What is your name?"

"My name is Man 44," the boy said quietly without opening his eyes.

"Do you know Boy 12?"

"No. I do not know Boy 12."

"Good." Merlynn patted his arm. "Man 44, you are a grownup now. You are no longer a boy so you will not live with the boys and go to school. You will live with the other men and go to work in the mine. I will give you more instructions when you wake up. Again, what is your name?"

"My name is Man 44."

"Who is the only person you will listen to?"

"I will only listen to you."

"You will do whatever I order you to do?"

"Yes." The boy nodded.

Merlynn smiled. "Very good, Man 44. You can go back to sleep now and I will speak to you later." Still sitting in the swivel chair, she wheeled herself toward Loren's chair on the other side of the room. "This one is really gonna be fun," she murmured, her grin widening.

Merlynn lifted herself out of the chair and approached the beautiful sleeping teen. She stroked the girl's blonde hair lovingly as she watched Loren's chest rise and fall rhythmically with each breath.

"Hello, dear," the woman said softly, leaning over the reclining chair. "My name is Merlynn and I am your leader. Whenever you hear my voice, you will immediately listen to me and do whatever I tell you to do." She caressed Loren's arm with her chubby fingers. "Do you understand?"

The girl nodded without opening her eyes.

"Answer me."

"Yes. I understand."

"That's better, dear." Merlynn patted the girl's hand. "What is your name?"

"My name is Loren Cofton."

"No, that is not correct. Loren Cofton is no longer your name. There is no Loren Cofton. I am giving you a new name now. Your new name is Woman 7 and that is the only name you will answer to. Now, tell me, what is your name?"

"My name is Woman 7."

"Who is Loren Cofton?"

"I do not know who Loren Cofton is."

"What is your name again?"

"My name is Woman 7."

Merlynn smiled at the girl, whose eyes remained closed. "You are doing very well, Woman 7. I am pleased with you. Now I will start to give you your instructions. Every woman in our town has a job and I have a wonderful job for you. When you wake up, you will work for me, in my house, as my personal servant. You will do whatever I tell you to do—dress me, wash me, kiss me, and much, much more. Do you understand?"

Loren nodded.

"Speak."

"Yes," the girl whispered. "I understand."

"You will kiss me?"

"Yes. I will kiss you."

"What a lovely thought, dear," Merlynn said as she caressed the girl's nipples. "And I will kiss you too. Now, tell me again, what is your name?"

"My name is Woman 7."

"Excellent, Woman 7. We'll talk again when you wake up. But right now I will give you one more important instruction that you must carry out when the time comes. Listen carefully..." Speaking very softly, Merlynn told the sleeping teen what she needed her to do.

After breakfast Saturday, Tracie left Brenda's apartment and, once again driving the Prius (one window still minus its glass), headed for Corsonia. In her pockets she carried a can of Mace and a knife, but hoped she wouldn't have to use the weapons, knowing that if she did, she'd probably wind up captured or killed, and, either way, the plan would fail. "Then Loren'll be a zombie forever," she mumbled.

She and Brenda had piled two cases of bottled water into the rear of the car, but that amount of untainted liquid wouldn't be nearly enough to supply all the people where she was going. She was counting on the pure water having been delivered and at least partly consumed by now.

Tracie sighed as she recalled yesterday morning's events. Luckily, she and Loren had finished their bottle switch before the sheriff had arrived and started shooting. But if he suspected what they had been doing there—or tortured Loren to make her talk—then it was all over.

She shook her head, trying to block out the negative thoughts. It was no use thinking about all the things that could go wrong; there were too many possibilities. She just had to be brave and positive, like Loren, and hope her friend had been right.

Anyway, she thought, *I'm gonna find out real soon.*

"She's not at the motel or, if she's in there, she's not coming out of her room, even to eat," Sheriff Dugan told Merlynn as he stood in her office Saturday morning. "I was parked outside all day and she never left—and no one delivered any food. The Jeep's still in the lot too. Maybe she's driving that other car, the silver one."

"Too bad you couldn't just get her," the woman said as she reached for the ever-present box of Hostess cupcakes. "It would have been nice and easy. But, not to worry; it'll still be all right because her friend, who used to be called Loren Cofton, is now one of our people. I've named her Woman 7, my favorite number. Do you remember the last Woman 7, Tom?"

The sheriff nodded.

"It was so sad that Doctor couldn't control her infection and we had to destroy her. But this new Woman 7 is also a blonde—younger and very pretty." Merlynn removed the cellophane covering from one of the cupcakes, took a large bite, and smiled. "She's going to be my personal servant as soon as she wakes up."

"What if the girl's friend goes to the Montello police and tells them what happened?"

"You think they'll believe her crazy story?"

"Well, her friend is missing so, even if they don't believe her, they'll have to look for the girl."

Merlynn laughed, holding her hand over her mouth to keep the cake crumbs from escaping. "You really think the cops'll come to Corsonia and spend a lot of time here looking for her? Don't forget how scared they are of our little Hippy Town." She shook her head. "They'll brush it off, do a quick search, find nothing, and that'll be the end of it."

"I hope."

"In fact, I bet she won't even go to the police. She's going to come back to Corsonia by herself to try to rescue my Woman 7—and that's what you've got to prepare for, Tom. When that girl comes back here, I want you to get her and bring her to me."

"Yes, Merlynn," Dugan said, bowing his head.

Driving as quickly as she could, Tracie traversed the empty roads of Corsonia until she reached the wooded hill leading to the mine. After parking the Prius in the bushes two-thirds of the way toward the top and shoving two bottles of water into her jeans, she climbed the rest of the hill on foot.

As Tracie approached the rear of the fence, near the spot where she and Loren had crawled through the opening, she saw the outline of one of the guards. The man sat on the ground outside the enclosure, contemplating the grass, with his rifle a few feet away.

This is it, she told herself. *Loren'd better've been right.* Before she had a chance to change her mind, she grabbed her can of pepper spray, held it behind her back, and stepped directly in front of the inattentive guard.

"Hello," she said, smiling at the handsome man with a curly brown ponytail who seemed to be in his mid-twenties. "How are you today?"

The man looked up and stared at her, an expression of utter bewilderment on his bearded face. "Who are you?" he asked, speaking with normal inflection in his voice, not a monotone. "What are you doing here?"

Exhaling in relief, Tracie continued to smile as she quickly answered him. "My name's Tracie and I wanted to see what was going on up here. What are you guarding with that rifle?" She pointed to his weapon. "And do you know what's inside the fence?"

The man shook his head. "I don't know anything," he said. "About an hour ago, I found myself standing out here, holding the rifle. But now I can't seem to remember why." He shrugged his shoulders. "I've just been sitting here, trying to figure it all out."

"I think I can help," Tracie said, shoving the Mace into her pocket and sitting next to him. "Here. Have a drink of water. It'll help to clear your head while I tell you what's been happening. It's going to sound very strange and disturbing, but, unfortunately, it's all true."

"Good morning," Merlynn said to the former Boy 12, whose expressionless eyes were now open. "How do you feel?"

"I feel fine."

"Great." She pushed her swivel chair closer to him and leaned over so she was just a few inches from his face. "And what's your name?"

"My name is Man 44," he said, speaking in a monotone.

"Excellent. As I told you, from now on you will be working in the mine with the other men and women. But it is too late for you to go there today so you will work in my house. I have some chores for you to do. After breakfast, you will sweep the garage until it is completely clean. Do you understand?"

"Yes. I will sweep the garage until it is clean."

"Very good. You will get started soon—Man 24!"

Seconds later, the tall thin servant limped into the laboratory, his dull eyes staring at Merlynn's face.

"Give Man 44 some breakfast. Then take him into the garage and get him a broom. He's going to clean the floor."

Man 24 nodded. "Come," he said.

The boy slid off the reclining chair and followed him.

"...and then we switched the whole supply of bottled water in the store and that's why you're talking to me instead of shooting me with that thing," Tracie said in conclusion, indicating the discarded rifle. "Something in the bottled water you've been drinking lets whoever's doing this control your mind."

The handsome young man stared at the ground, holding his head in his hands. "None of this makes any sense at all," he muttered.

"Then tell me why you're here, guarding a mine that you don't even remember."

"I remember this old mine being up here, but it was deserted. Hadn't been operating since way before I was born."

"Well, it's operating now, that's for sure. I was in it with my friend just a few days ago and that's where lots of the people in this town work."

"But I don't work. I'm just a kid." He lifted his head and looked at Tracie, a bewildered expression covering his face.

"I'm sorry, but you're not a child anymore. You've even got a beard. Did you know that?"

The young man fingered the hair on his chin. "How can all this have happened?" he murmured.

"We're going to find that out. I promise. But right now, I need some more information. What's the last thing you remember doing before you found yourself here?"

The man thought for a few seconds. "I was eating dinner at home with my family."

"What were you drinking?"

"Soda. We had these free bottles of soda and water my mom said was left by our door. A company was giving them away." He gazed at Tracie. "She said they were advertising some kind of new product."

"Do you remember the date?"

"It was a Thursday—April 19th, 2001."

Tracie looked at him sadly. "That was more than thirteen years ago," she whispered. "This is July—and the year is 2014."

The man's eyes started tearing. "I was just eleven-years-old. You mean now I'm twenty-four? I lost all those years of being a kid—going to school, having fun."

"I'm so sorry." She didn't speak for several minutes, giving him a chance to digest the disturbing information. "Do you have any idea who could have done this terrible thing?"

He shook his head. "I only remember up to that day in April. What about my family? My name's Matt Harrison and I've got a younger brother, mother, and father. What's happened to all of them?"

"I don't know, Matt. All the people here just have numbers for names—like Man 23 or Boy 11—and I think everyone lives together in groups like in a commune. My friend and I saw the boys' house and there must be another place like that for the girls. I don't know how the women and men live, but I bet it's not anything like regular families."

"How are we going to find the people who did all this?" Matt asked, standing up.

"My friend and I came up with a plan, so here is what we have to do now..." Tracie talked and Matt listened attentively.

Merlynn smiled as Loren opened her eyes and stared at her. "Hello, sweetie," Merlynn said, stroking the girl's left arm. "Do you remember me?"

"You are the leader," Loren said, speaking in a monotone.

"Very good, dear. And what is your name?"

"My name is Woman 7."

"Yes, it is, and you are very lucky, Woman 7, because that is my favorite name." Merlynn slid her pudgy hand from Loren's arm to the girl's upper torso and began tracing circles around her firm left breast.

Loren showed no reaction to the caresses as she continued to stare at Merlynn with dull eyes.

"I'm sure you'll be my favorite woman because you are really so lovely and so young. But you look much too serious. I don't like that. You must smile whenever you are with me, Woman 7."

"Yes. I will smile." Loren's mouth widened into a phony-looking grin.

"Not quite as big a smile."

The girl formed a smaller grin.

"That's much better, dear." Merlynn removed her hand from Loren's chest and slowly lifted herself from the chair. "All right, sweetie. We'll have plenty of time to enjoy each other later, but first you have to eat and then you need a good bath. You're very lovely, Woman 7, but you do reek from all that futile activity yesterday. Before I leave, tell me that you love me."

"I love you," Loren said robotically, her mouth shaped in a slight grin.

"How very sweet. And I love you too, Woman 7." Merlynn leaned over the reclining chair and kissed the girl firmly on the lips.

CHAPTER 18

Lance Kimbrough sat at his desk late Saturday morning trying to understand what was going on. For the first time since he'd been operating the mine, things weren't running smoothly. It had started when he'd taken attendance. Everyone had been there, but they'd almost all seemed a little different, sluggish, and somehow off.

For one thing, roll call had taken much longer than usual. The responses had been slow and, afterwards, the workers had moved lethargically into the shaft, as if they weren't sure of what they were supposed to do. Kimbrough shook his head. That was impossible. Most of these people had been laboring in the mine for years and they were all excellent workers. But a few of the men and women hadn't even changed into their mining uniforms and he'd had to direct them to the shack for their equipment. That had never happened before. *Very odd.*

He reached for the phone and picked up the receiver to call Merlynn. *But what do I tell her?* Maybe he could explain that the workers were acting strangely. *No.* Putting down the phone, he gazed out the window. *She'd just blame me, get angry, send Dugan...*

Holding his head in his hands, he leaned over the desk and tried to concentrate. *Got to do this by myself. Figure out what's wrong and then fix it.*

Tracie and Matt walked along the perimeter of the fence and found a gray-haired bearded and ponytailed man sitting on the ground, examining the weapon in his hands.

"What am I doing out here with a rifle?" the man asked, looking up as they reached him. "I don't know anything about guns. I'm a math teacher, not a soldier. I don't understand..." He shook his head in confusion.

"I'm going to try to explain," Tracie said, sitting next to him. "This is Matt and I'm Tracie."

"Jim Thornberry."

"Jim, this is gonna sound like it's impossible," Tracie continued. "But it's the truth. What's the last thing you remember doing?"

"My wife and I were eating dinner. But it's daytime now..."

"Do you remember what you were drinking?"

"Yeah. Some kind of new soda, a free sample pack that was left at our door when my wife came home. We decided to try it with dinner." He shrugged. "I don't remember anything after that."

"Sometime in April of 2001, right?" Matt asked.

"April 26th."

Tracie shook her head. "I'm sorry, but that day was a long time ago."

"What?" Jim asked incredulously.

"The year is now 2014. I'm so sorry."

"That's impossible."

"It's true," Matt said, fondling his beard. "I was just a kid and look at me now. I lost all those years too, Mr. Thornberry."

"Where's my wife?" the man said, standing up.

Tracie gazed at him sadly. "I don't know. But, I promise, we're gonna try to find her."

Sheriff Dugan drove several yards past the boys' school and parked his SUV on the side of the empty road. "Something's not right," he muttered as he stepped out, glancing at the rear of the school building.

The boys were in the backyard, talking, chasing one another, or throwing sticks. They were making a considerable amount of noise, yet no one was reprimanding them. *Where was the teacher? Was the man sick? What about the housekeeper?* She was programmed to alert him if there was any problem.

The boys should have been in class, learning whatever it was they were studying. It wasn't lunchtime yet. The kids were given a short recess after they ate, but not now. And they were never supposed to run loose by themselves, without supervision.

"I don't like this at all," the sheriff mumbled as he approached the front door of the house.

Tracie led Matt Harrison and Jim Thornberry to the loosened part of the bottom of the fence she and Loren had discovered on their first visit to the mine and the men stretched it so they were able to fit through the opening. Then, after all of them crawled underneath and pushed the rifles through, they continued walking down the hill toward the buildings.

"You say there's someone here in charge of all of this?" Matt asked, indicating the mine complex.

"Yes," Tracie said. "The man who took attendance and noticed me and my friend. But I don't know his name or exactly who he is."

"Is he the one who did this to us, took away all those years?" Jim asked. "Because if he is, I'll figure out how to shoot this thing." He pointed to the rifle he carried.

"I don't think so, Jim. He didn't seem at all like a leader to me. But I'm hoping he can tell us what's going on and who he's working for."

"Heck, I don't even need a rifle," Matt said. "I'll just put my hands around the man's neck and strangle him."

"Please," Tracie begged. "I understand how you guys feel. But we need to talk to this man and get him to tell us what he knows about how this terrible thing happened. I've still got to find my friend and both of you still want to find your families."

"Yeah," Jim mumbled. "But after that..."

They walked the rest of the way down the hill in silence.

Dugan opened the door to the boys' school and stepped inside. "Hello!" he called. "Teacher, where are you? Woman 28, come here! I need to talk to both of you—now!"

As the sheriff stood in the hallway waiting for a response, he could hear the boys playing noisily outside in the yard. But the interior of the house was totally silent and neither of the adults came forward.

Dugan walked into the large open space on the ground floor that served as the boys' classroom. The room looked as if it had been hit by a tornado. Chairs and tables were turned on their sides and textbooks, notebooks, pens, and pencils littered the entire floor. Several of the notebooks had been torn in half and pieces of paper had been ripped out and crumpled into balls.

"What the...?" Dugan mumbled as he stepped around the various obstacles, trying to figure out what had happened.

He dashed out of the classroom and quickly checked the rest of the house, finding nothing else out of place. Where were the teacher and the housekeeper? Could someone have kidnapped them? *But why?*

"Shit," he muttered as he walked to the backyard to question the boys. "This can't be good."

When Tracie, Matt, and Jim reached the mine complex at the base of the hill, they saw some of the workers lingering near the entrance to the shaft. A few sat on the ground talking quietly to one another; others stood by themselves, seemingly lost in their own thoughts.

"Should you go over there and tell them what's going on?" Matt asked Tracie.

"Later," she said. "But right now, I think we should find the man in charge." She pointed to the largest building. "Let's try over there. That one looks like it could be an office."

The three of them continued walking until they came to the entrance of a two-floor wooden house with a satellite dish on the roof. "If he's in here, I want both of you to aim your rifles at him," Tracie said.

"I told you, I don't even know how this thing works," Jim said.

"It doesn't matter. We just want to scare him into talking to us."

"I can fire a rifle," Matt said. "My dad taught me."

"No shooting, please. We need this man to tell us what he knows or we may never find your families, my friend, and all the other people who're missing. Okay?"

Matt nodded.

"All right then. Here goes." Tracie took a deep breath and banged her fist on the front door.

As soon as the six boys noticed Dugan in the yard, they immediately stopped playing and stood quietly, staring at him.

"What's going on here?" the sheriff asked.

None of the boys responded. They gazed in awe at the strange clean-shaven man, who looked and sounded different than the few adult males they knew.

"I asked you a question," he repeated.

The biggest boy, a freckle-faced redhead, took a step forward. "We were in school doing our work. Then Teacher told us to go."

"What?"

"Yes," a smaller boy agreed. "That is how it happened. Teacher said, 'Get out, now!' He said the words very loud so we were frightened and we all ran outside."

"When did this happen?"

The boys looked at each other and several shrugged. None of them wore a watch.

"We do not know the time," the big redhead said. "We have been here waiting for Teacher to tell us to return to school."

"What about Woman 28? Where is she?"

The redheaded boy shrugged. "I do not know. I have not seen Woman 28 since we went outside."

Dugan looked at the other five boys. "Have any of you seen her?" he asked.

Three of the boys muttered, "No" and two shook their heads.

"Did you boys turn over the tables and chairs in the classroom or rip up paper?"

All six children stared at the sheriff, confused expressions covering each of their faces.

So they hadn't made the mess. Dugan sighed. He couldn't send them back into the room until it was cleaned up. "Okay, then. You boys stay outside here and play until another grownup comes. Do not leave the yard. Is that understood?" He looked at the redheaded boy.

"Yes," the boy said, nodding vigorously.

The sheriff turned and rushed to his car. *Gotta find them. Can't have gone far on foot.*

Tracie banged her fist on the door of the building in the mine complex for the second time and again got no response. "Open the door!" she shouted.

"This isn't working," Jim said. "If someone's inside, he's not letting us in. We're going to have to break down the door. Come on," he told Matt.

The two men threw their bodies against the door and, after the third try, the door flew open and they fell forward into the hallway.

"What's all this?" Matt asked as he lifted himself and his rifle from the floor and stared at the large computer-filled room in front of him.

"It looks like some kind of a work station," Tracie said as she entered the building and walked into the spacious room. "But it's gotta have phone service so first I'm gonna make a call and see if we can get some help." She took out her cell phone and punched in a stored number. "Damn," she muttered as she listened to a recording. "No answer. I have to leave a message." She spoke into the phone and described the situation as best she could.

"Okay," she said, dropping the phone into her jeans pocket. "Now let's go see if the person this stuff belongs to is someplace here. Stick together, and Matt, be ready to point your rifle, just in case."

Matt nodded and he and Jim stood alongside Tracie as the three of them began searching the house.

The rest of the ground level consisted of a small galley kitchen, an eating area, and a sitting room. "There's no place anywhere down here to hide," Tracie said after they had examined the sparsely-furnished rooms and closet. If he's inside, he's gotta be upstairs." She indicated the central staircase.

"Me first," Matt said, thrusting his rifle toward the steps.

"Okay," Tracie agreed as she and Jim followed him to the second floor.

Sheriff Dugan drove slowly through the empty streets adjoining the boys' school, looking for the missing teacher and housekeeper. After traveling several miles, he stopped the car and walked outside, shaking his head. *Nothing. No sign of either of them.*

He stood alongside the car and considered his next step. He would have to report back to Merlynn. She needed to know the problem and assign someone to clean up the classroom and supervise the boys.

He gazed at the peaceful rural landscape. Nothing seemed different. *Where could those two be? And how the hell did they leave?* He sighed. Let Merlynn figure it out. After all, she was the genius behind this. If something was broken, she'd have to fix it. After stepping inside his SUV, he made a U-turn and headed for Merlynn's house.

Tracie and the two men began searching the second floor of the building in the mine complex. The first room they entered was a large bedroom.

Tracie opened the sliding doors of the closet and separated the jeans and shirts hanging inside. "A man definitely lives here," she said.

"But where is he?" Jim asked as he peered under the bed.

"You said this is some kind of mine," Matt said to Tracie. "So then maybe he's somewhere in there."

"Maybe," she agreed. "But don't give up on finding him here just yet. There're more rooms on this floor."

The three of them checked the bathroom—the tub was empty—and, as Jim and Matt aimed their weapons, Tracie opened the next door. They walked into a small den, which contained only a desk and plaid sofa.

Jim pulled out the two couch cushions. "No place to hide in

here," he said, shrugging.

Tracie indicated the remaining closed room. "Only one door left. Let's give it a try."

As the two men pointed their rifles, Tracie slowly turned the knob and swung the door open. The room was unfurnished, with two large cartons in the center.

"Just storage," Jim said dejectedly, sticking his hand inside the boxes and lifting a couple of science books.

"What about there?" Matt asked, indicating the closet.

As Tracie flung the closet open, the man crouching inside immediately raised his hands. "Don't shoot me, please!" he begged.

"Is this the guy you saw?" Matt, still aiming his rifle at the cowering man, asked Tracie.

"Yes." She turned to the thin man with glasses and a goatee. "What's your name?"

"Lance Kimbrough."

"And what do you do here?"

"I'm the supervisor of the mine. Please don't hurt me," Kimbrough whimpered as he stood up slowly, still holding his arms over his head.

"That's up to you if we hurt you," Tracie said. "We need you to tell us everything that's going on in this mine—the truth."

"Yes," Kimbrough said, bobbing his head. "I'll tell you whatever you want to know. Just don't shoot."

CHAPTER 19

The two people most recently known as Teacher and Woman 28 walked through the back streets of Corsonia early Saturday afternoon, not talking much, as they tried to figure out what had happened to them.

Teacher's real name was Arthur Slayton and he had been the office manager for a local lumberyard. When he had found himself in a classroom with a bunch of strange boys who called him "Teacher," he had been totally confused.

"I shouldn't have gotten mad at the kids and chased them out," he murmured. "And then throwing the furniture..."

"It's okay," his companion said. "I felt like throwing something too." The woman's real name was Pamela Chilvers and her last memory was of being a wife and the mother of two young girls.

Both of them had glanced in the mirror of the school's bathroom and been shocked at their altered appearances.

Arthur had last remembered being 32-years-old, but he now looked at least a decade older. His thin brown hair had receded so much that he was mostly bald. Yet, for some reason, the hair on the bottom of his head was long and he wore it in a ponytail. From what he could see under a shaggy beard, his face was heavily lined. Also, he had weighed nearly two hundred pounds and now probably tipped the scale at thirty pounds less. He liked to eat and didn't recall being on any diet.

Pamela thought she had aged much more than ten years. Her blonde hair had turned white and she wore it in a simple ponytail, something she had never done because the style was unflattering, accentuating the length of her long thin face. She wore no makeup, which, with her pale complexion, made her look like a ghost. Staring down at her clothes, she shook her head. The black tee shirt and polyester gray slacks she had on were definitely not items from her wardrobe. They were cheap, ugly, and much too loose.

Neither of them remembered how they had gotten into that school with the six strange young boys.

"The kids said I took care of the house," Pamela said. "But I don't work—I take care of my own house and my husband and my girls. Where are they?"

Arthur had been engaged to a young woman from Montello. *Did she leave him?* He couldn't remember having had any argument.

The two of them, who knew each other casually, had decided to walk to Pamela's house since it was just a little more than a mile from the small school building. As they traveled along the deserted streets, they were becoming more and more anxious: Where were all the cars and all the people? This was not the town they remembered. It was all wrong.

Tracie, Matt, and Jim listened incredulously to Lance Kimbrough's explanation.

"These people worked for you here for many years and you only knew them as numbers," Tracie interrupted. "Didn't you ever think that was weird?"

"Merlynn told me at the beginning that it would be easier to keep track of everyone that way. I never really thought much about it."

"What about the way they all looked—their eyes?" Matt asked. "Tracie said it's like zombies."

Kimbrough shook his head. "I guess they looked a little different." He gazed at the three of them sadly. "They were all very quiet. But I'm really not good with people so I didn't know anything was wrong. And they were such good workers."

"Because we were like robots!" Jim shouted. "Goddamn robots!" He put his head in his hands and sobbed. "Oh my God! Thirteen years. Thirteen goddamn years..."

No one spoke for several seconds. Then Tracie turned to Kimbrough. "This woman, Merlynn, you said she was in charge. She's the person responsible for everything here?"

Kimbrough shrugged. "I guess so. She's the one who hired me and started up the mine again. And then I thought she hired the miners."

"Where does she live?" Jim demanded.

"It's out of the way, but I can take you there."

"You bet you can," Matt said, shoving the rifle into Kimbrough's stomach. "I still can't believe you were dumb enough to think you were running a real mine."

"But it is a real mine. Everyone worked, did their job, and we produced a lot of gold. Please..."

Matt moved the rifle a few inches away, but still aimed it at Kimbrough's midsection.

"That's what this is all about," Tracie said. "Money. The gold. This Merlynn person must've wanted it all for herself." She glanced at Kimbrough. "The sheriff works for her, right?"

The geologist frowned at the thought of Dugan. "Yes."

"Anyone else?" she continued.

"I don't think so. I'm here nearly all the time so I can't really be sure."

Matt snarled at him. "You're a piece of shit. But you're probably right. Merlynn sounds too greedy to want to share this mine with a lot of other people."

"You know," Jim said softly. "I've been thinking about that unusual name ever since he mentioned it and I've heard it before. Merlynn...Merlynn Baxter. She was in college and her parents died in a car accident."

"Do you remember when that happened?" Tracie asked.

"Not too long before that last day in April. And this Merlynn—she was some kind of a whiz kid. When she was younger, she was in the papers and on the local news a lot."

"For what?"

"Chemistry."

"This is it," Pamela said when she reached a white two-story house with yellow shutters missing several slats and overgrown grass surrounded by untrimmed shrubbery. She stared sadly at the building and hesitated before walking closer.

"It's okay," Arthur said, taking her hand. "We'll do this together." He nudged her forward and the pair climbed the step to the front door. Arthur twisted the knob and the door opened.

As soon as they entered the hallway, Pamela waved her hands in front of her face. The stagnant air irritated her throat and she began coughing.

"It looks like no one's been here in years," Arthur said, running his fingertips through the heavy layer of dust on a glass cocktail table in the living room.

"This is my furniture," Pamela said when she was again able to talk. "But I was a good housekeeper." Gingerly, she lifted a dust-covered decorative pillow from the lime green sofa and examined it at arm's length before turning to Arthur. "You're right. Nobody's been inside this house for a long time—so what's happened to my family? Where'd they all go?"

Arthur shrugged. "I have no clue." He indicated the staircase. "Do you want to check upstairs? See if you find anything there that could help?"

"I guess we may as well since we're already here."

The two of them climbed the steps to the second floor.

Tracie frowned at Lance Kimbrough, who sat quietly in the chair they had shoved him into. "So Merlynn was a chemistry whiz kid," she said to Matt and Jim. "I think I'm getting a clearer picture of how she did all this."

"She must have put something in the drinks," Jim said, nodding. "She created some kind of chemical formula that let her control our minds—something so powerful that we can't even remember anything we did during all that time."

"For so many years straight?" Matt asked. "How could she do that?"

"Once she controlled you, she must have ordered you to drink her bottled water every day, keeping the drug in your body," Tracie explained. "When my friend and I switched her water supply yesterday, it kinda woke everyone up—like out of a deep trance."

Jim shook his head. "This is like something from a bad fairy tale."

"We gotta go there and get Merlynn," Matt said, raising his rifle.

"Yeah," Tracie agreed. "But she's real smart and real dangerous so we need lots more people than just the three of us." She smiled at Matt and Jim. "And I think I know just where we can find them."

"I'm afraid to go into these rooms," Pamela said to Arthur as they climbed the last step and stood in the hallway of the second floor of her house. "You go in first."

"It won't be so bad. I'm sure there's nobody here."

"Yes, and that's the problem."

"All right," Arthur said. "I'll check everything out." He pointed to the door on the left. "What's in this room?"

"That's our bedroom—Bill's and mine."

Arthur walked inside and, a minute later, returned to the hallway. "There's nothing much to see in there. It's just a dusty room that no one's been in for a long time. Take a look." Gently, he took Pamela's arm and propelled her forward.

She poked her head into the room and quickly moved back. "That's enough."

Arthur pushed open the door in the middle of the hall and glanced inside. "Nobody's used this bathroom in years either." He indicated the two doors on the right. "Are these your daughters' rooms?"

Pamela nodded.

Arthur stepped into the nearest room and came right out. "Maybe you shouldn't go in here. This one's kind of a mess."

Pamela peeked inside and saw a desk turned upside down, posters partially ripped off the wall, dresser drawers flung opened, and clothes dumped all over the bed and the floor. She put her hand in front of her mouth and muttered, "What do you think happened?"

"Looks like some kind of a fight. How old was your daughter the last time you remember seeing her?"

"Briana was eleven."

Arthur stood quietly for several seconds. "Let's look at the next room," he suggested. He entered the room and stayed inside for a couple of minutes.

"What're you doing in there for so long?"

"Just looking around. You can come in whenever you want. This one's fine. It's nothing like the other room."

Pamela entered her younger daughter's bedroom and glanced

at it. Although the once hot-pink walls were now dull and coated with dust, the room itself looked untouched. Crystal's collection of stuffed animals was intact. Each furry creature still stood in its assigned position in the large bookcase. Although her daughter had been just five-years-old, she was a neat child with a keen sense of order. Everything had to be in its rightful place.

Pamela felt a small sense of relief. Then she shifted her gaze to the girl's bed. "Oh no!" she moaned.

"What's wrong?"

Pamela rushed to the bed and scooped up the familiar white stuffed animal with the black nose and floppy ears. Then, holding the dusty toy against her chest, she turned to Arthur, her eyes brimming with tears. "Snoopy was Crystal's favorite. She never went anywhere without him."

After Tracie left a second phone message, explaining what she hoped to do and where she expected to be, she, Jim, and Matt sprung into action. Pushing Lance Kimbrough in front of them, they climbed down the staircase, left the building, and headed toward the mineshaft. As they walked, they passed various small groups of people, most still in their mining uniforms, huddled together and talking to one another.

Tracie approached each group and asked the people to follow her. "I think I'll be able to give you some answers," she said when the confused workers started questioning her about what they were doing at the mine, who the short guy with glasses and a goatee was, and why the two men she was with were pointing rifles at him. "I'll explain everything," she promised. "But first I need you to come with me so I can talk to everyone together."

Like the Pied Piper, she collected more and more people, all of them walking with her until they reached the shaft. Tracie sent several of the workers into the mine to round up the men, women, and children who were still inside and she dispatched another team to find the people who had been outside, guarding the fence. When all the workers had been collected, everyone formed a large semicircle around Tracie and the three men with her.

She gazed at the crowd and smiled at the people. "Hi," she began. "My name's Tracie Martinez. None of you know me because I'm not from around here."

"I know you," said a solemn voice from the back of the crowd.

Tracie recognized the voice and beamed. "Yes, you do," she said. "It's so good to see you again, Boy 11."

"Where is your friend?" he asked.

"That's part of what I have to tell you."

"What are you two talking about?" a man standing in the front shouted. "I just want to know what the hell I'm doing here! I found myself swinging an axe in that mine about an hour ago—and I don't remember how I got there."

"Yeah, me too!" a woman yelled.

"What's going on?" another man asked.

"Please!" Tracie shouted. "Just listen to me." She shoved Kimbrough in front of her and began to explain.

CHAPTER 20

With his hat in his hands, Sheriff Dugan stood in front of Merlynn's desk early Saturday afternoon, doing his best to explain the disturbing situation he had found in the boys' school.

"It sounds like those two didn't drink their water," Merlynn said, unwrapping a Hostess cupcake and taking a hefty bite. "Did you check the refrigerator?"

He shook his head. "It was so crazy there that I didn't think of it and, after I talked to the boys, I jumped right in the car to look for the teacher and housekeeper."

"But you couldn't find them." She let out a loud snort. "Some sheriff you are!"

Dugan stared at the floor, angry with himself for not thinking of inspecting the refrigerator and stung by Merlynn's criticism.

"Well, we can't worry about those two now," Merlynn continued, taking another mouthful of cupcake. "They won't get far on foot. I've just got to analyze how it could have happened. Either, for some reason, they didn't drink the water, or worse, they never even got their daily supply. When you captured my beautiful Woman 7 yesterday, weren't the two of them by the store?"

Dugan glanced up and nodded.

"Could they have tampered with the water?"

"I didn't see anything wrong. I did check the supply and all the bottles were inside the store, lined up right, and nothing was missing."

"Maybe they did something with the bottles before you got there. Too bad Woman 7's in no condition to tell us anything about what she and her friend did." She shook her head. "I really have to finish that compatible truth serum. But, right now, we have to assume the worst—that our people didn't get their water—and make plans. They'll be confused and won't understand what's going on. We've got to keep it that way until we can get them all back."

"What about Woman 7's friend—the brunette? She could be somewhere here, causing trouble."

"Don't worry about her." Merlynn shoved the last of the cupcake into her mouth and smiled at the sheriff with chocolate crumb-coated teeth. "That's been taken care of. Whenever the friend shows up, she won't be a problem."

After Tracie finished telling the miners what she believed had happened to the people in Corsonia, she was at first greeted by complete silence. Then, as if everyone realized the horror of the situation at the same time, the crowd erupted into furious shouts of rage. Several men and women headed toward Kimbrough, their fingers balled into fists. Matt still aimed his rifle at the geologist's midsection while Jim shooed the crowd away.

"Hold it!" Tracie yelled, waving her arms back and forth in an attempt to quell the incensed horde. "I know you've got lots of questions about your families and homes and everything else, but that'll have to wait till later. Right now, we've got to find this

Merlynn Baxter." She indicated the geologist, who stood cowering in front of her, looking at the ground. "According to Mr. Kimbrough, although he ran the mine, Merlynn's the one who set this whole thing up and made you work here, most of you for many years, so she's the one with all the answers."

Tracie stuck her finger into the geologist's side. "We need him 'cause he's gonna take us to her. We're going in my car and the rest of you can follow in the buses. There're three of them parked at the top of the hill. So, everyone, let's get out of here and go find Merlynn."

Pamela sat on the front step of her house, tears flowing down her cheeks, staring at the stuffed Snoopy she held tightly.

"I'm so sorry," Arthur said, sitting next to Pamela and putting his arm around the distraught woman's shoulders in a futile attempt to comfort her. "But maybe you're wrong about what you think happened and your daughter's really okay."

"No." She shook her head emphatically. "Someone took Crystal by force from her room. I'm sure of that." Wiping her tears with one hand, she looked up at him. "And I know they took Briana too, although she must've put up a strong fight. But all this must have happened a long time ago and I don't have any idea of how to find my girls now. And what about Bill? Where is he?"

Arthur sighed deeply and stood up, surveying the road. They hadn't seen either a car or another person since leaving the boys' school. But he didn't like the idea of just sitting and doing nothing. There had to be other people somewhere in the town. "Let's head to the stores," he suggested. "Maybe we'll find someone working there who can help us figure all this out."

"It's nearly five miles to the shopping center," Pamela said. "It's so hot out and I'm really tired."

"We need to get answers."

"I'm afraid of finding out what happened," Pamela whispered, standing and glancing back at her house. "It can't be anything good."

"Whatever it is, we have to know."

Pamela nodded and she and Arthur began walking toward the Corsonia stores.

Sheriff Dugan, with Man 24 sitting silently beside him, drove slowly through the empty streets of the town, still on the lookout for the missing teacher and housekeeper and any other disoriented residents who might have wandered away from their assigned places.

He had already visited the nursery and convinced the confused woman who cared for the babies to drink the water he carried, and then poured the bottles of water in her refrigerator down the sink. After he and Man 24 had dragged the sleeping woman into his car and he had taken her back to Merlynn to be reprogrammed—leaving Man 24 in temporary charge—he had driven one of Merlynn's female servants to the nursery to watch the infants. In the same trip, he had dropped a male servant at the boys' school to supervise the kids.

"Like a goddamn chauffeur service," he muttered as he and Man 24 headed toward the mine. He had called the geologist to warn him of a potential "problem" with the workers, but Kimbrough hadn't answered the phone. That wasn't unusual since the man spent most of his time underground, where he was impossible to reach.

The sheriff squirmed in his seat. He hated climbing into that mine—dark and creepy, like an open tomb. But most of the people of Corsonia worked there and they were probably in need of repairs. He carried the cure to their ailment in the storage compartment of his black SUV: ten cases of Merlynn's bottled water.

Pamela and Arthur headed for the main shopping center of Corsonia with Pamela leading them through the back roads, which she insisted was the quickest and most direct route.

She still carried Snoopy, glancing at the toy every few minutes and stroking it lovingly. "I'm getting real thirsty," she said, stopping in front of an empty field. "I finished my water a while ago."

"Here. Have some of mine." Arthur handed Pamela one of the two bottles he had taken from the refrigerator in the boys' school. "But this is the last one so don't drink it all."

Pamela placed Snoopy carefully on the grass and took a long sip. After wiping her mouth, she handed the bottle back to Arthur. Then she picked up the stuffed animal and the two of them continued walking toward the group of stores.

Sheriff Dugan drove up the hill to the mine entrance and reached the front gate, preparing to unlock it. But the fence was already open, the heavy chains lying on the ground. "I don't like this," he muttered.

Man 24, in the passenger's seat, made no comment.

Dugan drove into the parking area, which was empty except for Kimbrough's gray SUV. "Where are all the buses?" he mumbled.

Again Man 24 said nothing.

The sheriff, running as quickly as he could, dashed to the bottom of the hill toward the mineshaft. "Kimbrough!" he shouted. "What's going on here?" His booming voice resounded through the sleeping valley.

No one answered.

"Kimbrough!" the sheriff repeated. "Where are you? Where's everyone?"

Still hearing no response, Dugan darted into the opening of the shaft. "Kimbrough?" he called. "Anyone down there?"

The sheriff turned to the servant who had accompanied him

silently down the hill. "Man 24, go inside, take the elevator to the bottom, and see if you can find any people," he ordered.

"Yes," the man said, nodding as he immediately stepped into the mine.

Dugan raced to the geologist's house and pushed open the unlocked door. "Kimbrough!" he shouted again. "You in here?" The sheriff walked inside, glancing at the office and other ground floor rooms. Nothing seemed out of order, but the place was empty. *Where had Kimbrough and all the miners gone?*

Shaking his head, he took out his cell phone and called Merlynn.

Pamela sat on the ground in front of the vacant Commerce Bank of Nevada with Snoopy on her lap and wrapped her head in her arms. "I can't move another inch and I'm dying of thirst," she said, glancing up at Arthur who stood nearby. "Are you sure there's no more water?"

He shook his head. "You drank the last of it a few minutes ago. There's nothing left."

"So what're we going to do now? This center looks just like everything else in Corsonia. These stores have all been closed for a very long time."

Arthur sat next to her. "I think we should go over to 766 and try to flag down a car before it gets dark. There's got to be people someplace around here who can help us figure out what's going on."

"You're right. Maybe in a little while. But right now, I'm so tired and thirsty that I just need to stay here and rest." Still holding Snoopy, Pamela closed her eyes and lowered herself onto the weedy grass.

Talking to Merlynn on his cell phone, the sheriff described the perplexing scene he had found at the mine complex. "They're all missing—Kimbrough, the mineworkers, and the buses," he explained. "Only his car is there."

There was a pause before the woman spoke. "They couldn't have done anything without outside help. Even without my water, after so many years of not using their brains, those people are in no condition to make decisions by themselves."

"Maybe that dark-haired girl's responsible," Dugan suggested. "The friend who got away."

"It's possible. Or maybe our geologist friend suddenly turned into a boy scout. We won't know for sure what happened till we find them. Listen, Tom, before you and Man 24 come back here, do one last sweep of the town—just in case that's where they all are. Big yellow buses should be easy to spot."

"What if those buses go to Montello?"

"They don't have enough gas to get there."

"They could fill them."

"We control the only gas station in town and there's nothing along the way."

"Okay, say the buses stop in town and I find them," Dugan said, nodding his head. "What do I tell the people? They're all gonna be mad."

"No," Merlynn said. "You're wrong about that. They don't know what's going on so they won't be mad. But they are going to be confused—and probably thirsty."

"In that case..."

"...you should have no problem," she said, finishing the sheriff's sentence.

Pamela was half asleep when she heard a mechanical rumbling in the distance. "Is that a car?" she asked, immediately rising and opening her eyes.

"I think so—and it's heading this way," Arthur said as he dashed toward the road. "Come on and let's see if whoever it is can help us."

The two of them stood next to the street, waving their arms, as a black SUV approached and then stopped. Two people were inside the vehicle, but only one man stepped out.

"Howdy," the squat brown-haired man wearing black-framed eyeglasses and a Stetson said as he walked toward them flashing a huge smile. "How're you two folks doing today?"

"That's the problem," Arthur said. "We don't know how we're doing or what's going on. We found ourselves in some kind of a boys' school and the boys said we both worked there. But we don't remember anything about it." He nodded at Pamela. "And my friend here just visited her home and it's deserted. No one's been there in a long time and she thinks someone took her kids..."

"I *know* someone took them," Pamela interrupted, still hugging Snoopy tightly in her arms. "I need to find my family—my girls and my husband. Someone did something to them, to us—and to this town. Where are all the people? All the stores?" She indicated the empty buildings.

"Yes, I know," the man agreed, shifting to a serious expression. "Something is very wrong and that's why I'm here—to check everything out." He reached into his jeans pocket, took out his badge, and showed it to Arthur and Pamela. "See, I'm a sheriff—been assigned by the governor to investigate the situation in Corsonia." He smiled at them again. "Name's Thurstan—Sheriff Thurstan." *Glad I remembered to wear the disguise*, Dugan thought. *They could've recognized me.*

"Thank God!" Pamela cried, thrusting her arms into the air. "We're saved!" She grabbed Arthur and gave him a hug.

"You folks look awfully tired," Dugan said. "Did a lot of walking, huh?"

 Arthur nodded.

"Bet you're both hungry and thirsty too."

"You've got water?" Pamela asked.

"Of course," the sheriff said. "Step into the car and I'll grab a bottle for each of you. Then, while we drive to my temporary headquarters, I'll tell you everything that I've found out."

"You know where my husband and daughters are?" Pamela asked.

"Yes."

"And I need to find my fiancée," Arthur said.

"Of course." Dugan opened the rear door and watched as the teacher and housekeeper climbed inside. Then he lifted the back, removed two of Merlynn's bottles, and gave one to each of his new passengers.

As he settled into the driver's seat, he heard the caps being twisted and, staring into the rear mirror, he saw the man and woman in the backseat both take large gulps. "That's good," he murmured. "You folks just relax and, very soon, everything will be perfectly clear."

CHAPTER 21

"Let me know right before we reach her house," Tracie told Kimbrough as she glanced at the geologist through the car's rear-view mirror.

"Yes," Kimbrough said from the back seat. "I will." His hands were bound together with a belt donated by one of the miners and Matt, rifle still pointed, sat next to him.

They drove quietly for several minutes along the empty dirt road until Kimbrough spoke again. "Turn left at the next fork and then the house will be about five hundred yards ahead—on the top of the hill."

"What's with all the hills here?" Tracie muttered as she turned the Prius into the long driveway leading to Merlynn's house, the three buses following closely behind. "We're gonna have to park somewhere down here or she'll see us coming. The yellow buses are kind of hard to hide."

The mountainous trail was surrounded by brush and small scrubby trees. Tracie drove a few feet past a fairly large clearing and shoved the car into some of the bushes. "C'mon," she said to Jim, who sat next to her. Quickly, the two of them stepped outside and directed the buses to park in the open area.

Then, after all the people got out, Tracie stood on the top step of one of the buses and spoke to them. "Okay, everyone," she began. "We're here. Merlynn, the woman I told you about, that we all want to see, lives at the top of this hill and we're gonna walk up there and make her tell us exactly what she did and where your missing relatives and my friend are. But first, this is what I need you to do."

Merlynn hung up her office phone and grabbed a Hostess cupcake. She was glad Dugan had found the teacher and Woman 28 and had been able to take care of them. But the sheriff still couldn't answer the most important question: What had happened to Kimbrough and the rest of her people? *Where the hell were they?*

She took a large bite of the cake, waddled out of the office, and continued along the lengthy hallway, eating as she walked. By the time she reached her spacious laboratory, she had finished the snack.

Merlynn continued to the window-filled wall that overlooked the hill and stared into the distance. Was she in danger? *No.* She shook her head. The people, awakening from their lengthy stupor, wouldn't have the necessary brainpower to figure out what she had done. Even if they were temporarily out of her control, they weren't capable of planning and carrying out an attack.

But what about Kimbrough? The geologist knew where she lived. Would the man be foolish enough to bring the workers here? *Why would he?* He had a good thing going—and he disliked people; he loved only those rocks.

The girl? Woman 7's friend? Could she be involved? How much did she know? Merlynn shook her head. It was useless to guess the answers to so many impossible questions. She turned away from the windows and smiled. No matter what was going to happen, she would prevail—like she always did.

With Kimbrough leading the way—his hands still tied—Matt, Tracie, and Jim marched up the hill leading to Merlynn's house, with nearly all the former mine workers following closely behind. Boy 11 and the other two children had been ordered to remain below and guard the buses.

They moved relatively quietly for such a large group, not talking to one another. The only sounds were scraping noises made by their footsteps on the pebbly terrain.

"Stop right here," Tracie ordered Kimbrough as soon as the outline of the large multi-story house became visible.

Jim motioned everyone behind him to stop, and, like an obeying army, the men and women came to an almost immediate halt.

"Maybe we should go around to the back, just in case she's got guards posted in the front," Tracie whispered to Jim and Matt. "What do you guys think?"

"She's probably got people covering the back of the house too," Jim said. "Whichever way we approach, she'll be able to see us coming. There's no place here to hide." He pointed to the scrubby bushes and small rock outcroppings and shrugged.

"Then let's just go right at her," Matt suggested. "We've got the numbers."

"Yeah," Tracie agreed. "We do. But after what's happened to everyone here, I'd hate for any of them to get hurt now."

"Do we have a choice?" Jim asked.

"I guess not," Tracie said. "Okay. Let's do this."

Jim turned and signaled for the group to move forward again and they continued climbing the steep hill toward the imposing house.

Merlynn opened her front door and gingerly stepped outside. "Do you hear anything?" she asked the first guard she encountered.

"No," the young man replied, without turning to look at her. His expressionless eyes continued to stare straight ahead.

"Be sure to let me know the moment you hear or see something unusual."

"Yes," the man said, nodding his ponytailed head.

Merlynn stood next to the entrance for another minute. Then, satisfied all was well, she reached for the door. But as soon as she touched the knob, she heard a noise.

"Did you hear that?" she asked, grabbing the guard's arm.
"Yes."

She listened again and the sound seemed to be intensifying. It was a familiar noise, the patter of footsteps—lots of them—coming from the bottom of the hill. Still gripping the guard, Merlynn spun him around so he had look at her. "As soon as you see the first one—you know what you have to do."

The man nodded. "Yes."

"Good. Now watch carefully and I'm going to alert the others." Merlynn, moving as quickly as she could, headed to the next guard.

Tracie and the silent army marched up the hill with Kimbrough leading the way. The geologist had been unable to maintain his balance with his hands tied and kept stumbling so Tracie had instructed Jim to remove the bindings. "But don't try to run. If you do, they'll shoot," she had warned, indicating Matt and Jim, who still carried their rifles.

"I won't," Kimbrough had assured her.

Halfway up the hill, Tracie nudged Jim and pointed to the house. "I see someone there," she whispered.

Jim yanked Kimbrough's arm, pushing the man heavily to the ground and turning toward the people who followed, again signaling them to stop. He scrambled back to Tracie's side and looked where she had pointed. "Yeah," he said, nodding his head. "It's a guard and he's got a rifle. There must be others stationed around the house."

"We've got more people."

"But they've got more guns."

"Some of our people took axes from the mine."

"But those weapons won't do any good from this distance."

"Do we have another choice?"

Jim shrugged. "Not that I know of."

Be brave like Loren..."Then let's go."

As soon as one of Merlynn's stony-faced guards stationed at the front of the house saw a man approaching, he did as he was ordered. He reached for his weapon, removed the pin, and tossed the grenade in the direction of the first climber. Although his aim was accurate, the guard didn't have the necessary arm strength to quite reach his target. As a result, the bomb landed several yards in front of the man before it detonated.

But, as the guard watched, the explosion lifted the first man on the hill and tore him apart—his arms and legs separating from his torso and flying in different directions. When the noise stopped, the guard picked up another grenade and scanned the hill for the next invader, his blank expression never changing.

"Oh God!" Tracie shouted as she and the others lay on the hill, having instinctively fallen to the ground with the deafening roar of the nearby blast. "What was that?"

"Some kind of bomb—probably a grenade," Jim said.

"Did it hit anyone?"

Jim didn't answer immediately. "The guy who took us here—

the one who ran the mine—he's dead."

Tracie sighed. "Was anyone else hurt?"

Still lying on the ground, Jim shifted his body so he was able to stare at the scene around him. "I don't think so, unless they were hit by some of the shrapnel. We were very lucky the bomb didn't reach us."

She turned to Matt on her other side. "Can you shoot them?"

He shook his head. "They're too far away—and I'd have to stand up."

"Okay, then," Tracie said. "We need another plan and I think I might have an idea."

As he drove toward the dirt road that led to Merlynn's secluded house, Sheriff Dugan jumped in surprise at the sound of the nearby explosion. But he was the only one in the car who reacted to the sudden loud noise. In the seat next to him, Man 24 continued to gaze straight ahead, his face showing no expression; in the rear, both passengers lay across each other, arms intertwined and sleeping soundly. Nothing would rouse them for at least another ten hours.

Dugan stopped the car and rested his head on the steering wheel, closing his eyes. *What now?* Merlynn must be in some kind of trouble. *Should he call her?* Couldn't. No signal here. *Should he just drive there and try to help?* He shook his head. *No.* Too dangerous.

The sheriff shifted the car into reverse, made a U-turn and headed in the opposite direction, away from Merlynn's mansion. He didn't know yet where he was going—but wherever it was, it would be nowhere near this place.

Merlynn sat in her office listening for the sound of the next grenade blast. As she waited, she called Dugan, but got no answer. After leaving a message for the sheriff, she reached into the drawer of her desk and put an object into the pocket of her muumuu. She patted herself to make sure everything else she needed was in place. Then, hearing no new explosions, Merlynn walked toward the front of the house and, fearful of standing too close to a window, ordered the nearest guard to come inside.

"Why aren't you firing at the intruders?" she asked Man 44, the former Boy 12.

"I do not see the people on the hill anymore."

"But I heard a grenade several minutes ago."

The lanky boy nodded his head. "Yes. The guard next to me threw it. There was a man on the hill."

"And what happened to that man?"

"He is dead."

"Good. But where are all the other people?"

Man 44 shook his head. "I do not know."

She stared at him for a moment before speaking. "Go back to your post," she finally said. "Look carefully—and kill any person you see coming up the hill."

The young guard nodded and walked outside.

Doesn't make sense, Merlynn thought as she locked the door and headed to her laboratory at the rear of the house. *They wouldn't give up so fast.*

Tracie and her makeshift army moved very slowly up the hill, approaching from all sides. But, this time, they crawled on their knees, each person holding part of a bush in front of his or her body as a kind of superficial camouflage.

Tracie had suggested the idea to Jim and Matt when they had all retreated further down the hill after the grenade blast, explaining that the mind-controlled zombies she had encountered didn't use their brains at all. "They just do what they're told without thinking so they won't be able to see us if we disguise ourselves," she said.

"But we can't really hide completely," Jim argued. "They can see us through the bushes."

"I'm betting that, if we move slowly enough, they'll just notice a bunch of green bushes, not people."

"Even if you're right, what about that woman—Merlynn?" Matt said. "If she's there, she'll know what's going on."

"Yeah," Tracie agreed. "She will. But if we can get close enough before she notices us, this could work."

Now the army of mine workers, transformed into a spotty forest of mobile greenery, inched steadily up the hill until they were again within the view of the posted guards. But this time no grenade was launched and no shots were fired, allowing the bush-covered people to continue their crawl-march to Merlynn's house.

Merlynn, walking as quickly as her body allowed, trudged to her lab and headed toward the rear windowed wall. Peeking cautiously outside, she immediately saw the people, holding bushes in front of them, approaching steadily up the hill from all directions.

Since, for security purposes, her house didn't have a rear door, Merlynn returned to the front, moving as fast as she could and shouting orders to the remaining inside servants. Then she opened the door and again summoned the nearest outside guard.

"The...people...on...the...hill," she gasped, completely out of breath. "They're...nearly...here."

"I do not see any people," the bearded man said.

Merlynn grabbed the guard by his throat. "You idiot!" she yelled, nearly choking him. "They're hiding behind bushes!" She released him and he fell backwards, sliding across the hall floor. "Get back out there and start shooting at all the moving bushes. They're too close for the grenades. You'll blow up the house so just use the rifle. Tell the other guards to do the same. Now go!"

Without showing any emotion, the man stood and returned to

his outside post. "You must use the rifle to shoot the bushes moving on the hill," he immediately said to the guards on both sides of him. "Tell the others." Then, picking up his rifle, he aimed it at the nearest moving bush.

Tracie heard the sound of a bullet whizzing over her head, followed immediately by a man's cry of pain. "They're firing the rifles," she called to Jim, who was next to her on the hill. "No more crawling. We have to run right at them." She turned to the people behind her, yelling as loudly as she could. "Everybody! Take your weapons and get to the house as fast as you can—Now!"

The bush-camouflaged army threw down their greenery and began racing up the hill, charging quickly. From their posts surrounding the house, the guards fired at the onrushing swarm of men and women, hitting several, who crumpled and fell to the ground. But the rest of the people continued to surge forward.

Matt stopped and aimed his rifle at one of the guards, hitting the woman's shoulder. The wounded guard grasped her arm in pain and dropped her weapon.

Tracie and Jim, leading the charge, reached the entrance first. As a guard pointed his rifle at them, Tracie lunged at the man's stomach, knocking him backwards before he had a chance to shoot. She grabbed his rifle while Jim tugged at the front door.

"It's locked!" he cried.

Matt reached them and pushed Jim aside. "Let me," he said, pumping several shots into the keyhole. Then Matt twisted the knob and opened the door.

As they entered the house, Tracie heard signs of an ongoing battle outside—Merlynn's guards firing their rifles and the members of her army using axes and even their bare hands to overpower them. *So sad,* she thought, listening to the cries of agony. *Good people getting hurt. But this is war...*

CHAPTER 22

As she stood pressed against the corner of the inner wall of her laboratory, avoiding the danger of being seen through the rear windows, Merlynn could hear sounds of the battle being waged outside the house—rifle shots, screams, grunts, thuds. Whenever she peeked at the glass to catch a quick glimpse of the action, she saw men and women charging up the hill, ferociously attacking her armed guards and, in many cases, overpowering them.

"This was not supposed to happen," she mumbled, shaking her head angrily. "My people..." She edged along the wall, sidled her hefty body toward the door, and leaned into the hall. "Woman 7!" she shouted. "Come here, now!"

A moment later, Loren, dressed in a pair of ragged jeans and a tight black tee shirt that accentuated her firm breasts, entered the room. Although the girl's mouth was shaped into a smile, her blank eyes stared vacantly at Merlynn.

"Do you remember your orders?" the woman asked.

"Yes."

"Good. It's almost time so you must be ready."

"I am ready," the girl said, speaking the words with no inflection.

"All right then, Woman 7." Merlynn caressed the girl's shoulder before lowering her hand to gently cup each breast. "Give me a kiss before you go."

Loren moved closer to the woman and softly kissed her lips. Merlynn wrapped her muumuu-covered arms around the girl and returned the kiss with passion, thrusting her tongue deep into Loren's mouth. When she was finished, Merlynn smiled and fingered the docile servant's long blonde hair. "Bye, sweetie," she said, finally removing her hands from the girl's body. "No more time to play."

Loren bowed her head slightly and stepped into the hall.

The house was eerily quiet. Tracie, Matt, and Jim all held rifles as they strode through the long hallway, hearing only the sounds of their own footsteps. "Where is she?" Matt whispered.

Tracie shrugged. She peered into an open room, which contained shelves of books and a couch, but no people.

Jim slowly turned the knob of another room, kicked the door open, and quickly stepped back. Just as he did, a rifle blasted, the bullet whizzing a few inches from his right side. A young girl, her pale blonde hair in a ponytail, stepped forward and prepared to shoot again. But before she could do so, Matt knocked the weapon out of her hand and Jim grabbed it.

The girl lay on the floor of the small bedroom and stared at the three of them, her gray eyes registering no emotion.

"She's even younger than me," Tracie said to Matt and Jim. "Only thirteen or fourteen." She turned to the robotic girl and asked, "Why did you shoot at us?"

"It was an order." The teen's voice had no inflection.

"Are there more people with rifles inside the house?" Tracie continued.

"I do not know."

"Where is Merlynn?"

"I do not know," the girl repeated.

"This isn't helping," Jim said. "She's been programmed and can't tell us anything. We have to figure there are more of them hiding in some of the other rooms."

"Kinda like a video game with bombs going off," Matt said.

"Yeah," Jim agreed. "But this is for real."

Tracie nodded toward the girl, who still lay on the floor, gazing at them with empty eyes. "What do we do with her?" she asked.

"Better tie her up, just in case she's been ordered to do something else," Jim said. He opened the top drawer of a small bureau and pulled out a couple of long-sleeve shirts. "This ought to do it."

As Tracie, Jim, and Matt continued along the hallway, they heard the front door slam, followed by loud voices. "I think some of our people have gotten past the guards," Tracie whispered.

"Good," Jim said softly. "The more the..."

Before he could finish his sentence, a white-bearded short man popped out of a room a few yards in front of them, stepped into the hallway, and aimed a rifle in their direction.

"Duck!" Tracie shouted and they dropped to the ground. The bullet sailed over their heads and ricocheted off the wall at the other end of the corridor.

Matt scurried along the floor and tackled the shooter's legs, knocking him to the ground, minus his rifle. "What do you want me to do with Santa?" he asked as he lay on the man's chest, pinning his arms. The prisoner stared at the ceiling, not struggling, and showed no emotion.

"Toss him back in there and I'll tie him up," Jim said, indicating the open door. "At least these shooting robots don't move too fast."

As Jim finished binding the bearded prisoner's hands with the man's own belt, they heard another gunshot toward the front of the house, followed by sounds of a scuffle.

"I hope the good guys won," Matt said.

Tracie looked at him and shook her head. "Don't forget that they're all good guys, Matt, and they don't want to hurt us. It's that woman, Merlynn, who changed them, you—and everyone else she could. She's got my friend too."

"Yeah," Matt muttered. "Sorry."

"We're almost at the end of the hallway," Tracie said. "There's just one more door up the steps ahead."

As Tracie's group reached the end of the corridor, three men and two women joined them.

"Glad you made it," Tracie said, smiling.

"Many others will be here soon," a tall and gaunt bearded man, holding a bloodstained axe, said. "More people are getting through and coming into the house."

Jim climbed the steps, stood to the side of the door, and twisted the knob several times. "Another locked door," he said.

"Move away," Matt ordered. When the entrance was clear, he shot the lock, opened the door, and the band of invaders walked into the spacious laboratory.

"Welcome." Merlynn greeted the group from her swivel chair behind the cluttered worktable. "How nice of you all to come and visit."

Tracie moved forward and pointed her rifle at the woman's face. "Where's Loren?" she demanded.

"Oh, you miss your little friend. How sweet."

"Let me just shoot her now," Matt said, thrusting himself in front of Tracie and pressing the barrel of his rifle against the woman's wide chest.

"Then you'll never find your little friend. Very sad." Merlynn shook her head.

"No, Matt," Tracie said, pushing him away. "I have to get Loren first." She looked into the woman's stony green eyes. "What have you done to her?"

"And what do I get if I tell you?" Merlynn indicated the people behind Tracie. Another group of men and woman had entered the room, followed by sounds of approaching footsteps. "You've brought in all these people who want to kill me."

"How can you blame them after what you did?" Tracie asked.

Merlynn shrugged. "I kept them safe."

"You took away our lives!" a woman screamed. "You're a monster!"

Tracie dropped her rifle and moved closer. Pressing both arms on the table, she leaned forward and shouted in Merlynn's face. "Give me my friend!"

"Only if you let me go." Merlynn spoke quietly and smiled pleasantly at the enraged girl.

"You know I can't do that!"

"Then no deal."

"That's enough talk!" the gaunt man with the axe yelled. "Now you all step away so I can bash her brains in!"

Merlynn frowned at the man, but said nothing.

"I can't hold them back much longer so you may as well tell me where Loren is," Tracie said.

Merlynn shook her head.

The people behind Tracie surged forward, pinning the girl against the table. Slowly, the obese woman lifted herself out of her chair and waddled toward the rear of the room, next to the windows. The crowd followed and formed a half circle, those with axes aiming the weapons at her.

"Look at me," Merlynn wailed. "A poor helpless woman surrounded by a lynch mob. If you kill me, it would be murder."

"We won't kill you," Tracie said. "But we are gonna bring you in and then you're gonna go to jail for all the terrible stuff you did."

"No!" a woman in the crowd yelled. "She's gotta die for what she's done to us!"

"This is America!" Tracie shouted back. "We can't just kill her!"

While Tracie and her army members argued about Merlynn's fate, the fat woman reached into the pocket of her red and yellow flowered muumuu and extracted a nine-millimeter pocket pistol. She fired several rounds at the crowd, hitting Jim in the chest and a middle-aged woman standing behind him, both of them toppling to the floor. Tracie immediately dropped to the ground and crawled to her wounded comrade.

Meanwhile, Matt aimed his rifle at Merlynn. His bullet grazed her right arm, causing the woman to flinch in pain and drop her gun. As she glared menacingly at Matt, blood seeping from her wounded limb, someone in the crowd threw a stone. It bounced off the top of Merlynn's left shoulder before crashing loudly through the window behind her. Then another person hurled a second rock.

"Oww!" Merlynn winced as the stone smashed into her chest.

Some people continued to throw the rocks they had brought with them from the bottom of the hill, following Tracie's order, while others lifted vials and bottles from the worktable and counters and flung the glass containers at the cowering woman. The gaunt man stepped forward, his axe hoisted and vengeful eyes focused on his target.

"Don't kill her!" Tracie yelled from the floor where she still sat, cradling Jim's motionless head.

But the crowd drew closer to Merlynn, who leaned against the windows, ducking as best she could to avoid the bombardment of missiles. Then the gaunt man rushed at her, swinging his axe.

As she tried to avoid the blade, Merlynn lost her balance and fell backwards. "Woman 7!" she shouted, just before crashing through the broken window. She plummeted nearly twenty feet, her muumuued arms billowing like wings before she hit the ground and tumbled down the hill, only stopping when her clothing became entangled in the shrubbery.

People gathered along the shattered rear window and peered outside. "She's gotta be dead," the man with the axe murmured.

"Yeah," a tall woman next to him agreed. "She's just lying there, spread out in the bushes, like a big fat blob of flowers. Good for the bitch."

Tracie remained seated on the bloodstained floor, still cradling Jim's head. "Matt," she called, tearfully. "He's not moving."

As Matt turned from the window and walked to Tracie, he saw a blonde teen in a tight black tee shirt quietly enter the room, limping heavily on a bandaged left leg. "Look," he said, pointing to the doorway. "Is that your friend?"

Tracie lowered Jim's head gently to the ground and rose to her feet. "Loren!" she shouted. "Thank God, you're okay!" Tracie held out her arms and headed toward the girl.

Without speaking, Loren continued walking slowly to Tracie. When she reached Tracie, who stood smiling with her arms extended, Loren stepped into the embrace. Then, with Tracie's arms still wrapped around her, Loren withdrew a steak knife from her jeans pocket and stabbed her friend in the stomach.

"What're you doing?" Tracie shouted as she fell to the floor, the blade still wedged in her abdomen and blood gushing from the wound.

Without answering, Loren knelt down next to Tracie, quickly extracted the knife and tried to stab the girl again. But this time, Tracie rolled out of the path of the weapon and the blade hit only ceramic tile, the impact jolting it out of Loren's hand.

Before Loren could reach the knife, Matt and another man rushed forward and tackled her, pinning the girl to the ground. She lay quietly, neither struggling nor speaking.

"How bad is it?" Matt asked, letting go of Loren and squatting next to Tracie.

"I don't know," Tracie said, putting her hand on her stomach to staunch the blood flow. "It hurts..."

A petite Asian woman with a gray-streaked ponytail stepped through the group of people and spoke to Tracie. "I'm a doctor," she said. "Or at least I used to be before all this happened, so let me take a look." After she examined the wound, the woman applied a makeshift bandage using a tee shirt. "You're going to be fine," she said, smiling at Tracie. "Luckily, the knife didn't hit any vital organs."

Tracie glanced at Loren. Someone had tied the girl's hands behind her back with a belt and she now stood silently, staring blankly into space with expressionless eyes. "She's just like all the others—a robot. I should've figured."

"You were so glad to see her that you didn't think," Matt said, patting her hand. "But she'll be okay soon."

"And Jim?" Tracie asked.

Matt shook his head sadly.

As Tracie's eyes began to tear, she heard the faint sounds of sirens.

CHAPTER 23

"I got your messages, but it took forever to find this place," Brenda Hartwig said to Tracie as two medics lifted the girl into a stretcher, preparing to load her into one of the three ambulances parked in front of Merlynn's mansion. "I'm so sorry, hon." She reached for Tracie's hand and squeezed it.

"That's okay, Brenda," the girl murmured. "I'm just glad you're here." She closed her eyes to escape the glare of the spinning lights atop the nearby emergency vehicles. The noise produced by the scurrying personnel disturbed her too, but she couldn't drown it out.

"You just rest and get better, honey. It looks like you've had a really long day."

"Yeah," Tracie agreed, her eyes still closed. "Very long..."

Law enforcement officers and medical workers from Montello and other surrounding towns had converged on the battlefield early Saturday afternoon. Flashing red lights were everywhere as the police assessed the crime scene, rounded up the remaining zombies, and conducted interviews with Tracie and her army.

Meanwhile, EMTs attended to the wounded and retrieved the dead, which included Lance Kimbrough, Jim Thornberry, and five others. Merlynn, however, wasn't one of them. Somehow, the woman had disappeared. The police were searching the surrounding woods, theorizing that, in her weakened condition, she couldn't have ventured very far.

As the medics lifted Tracie's stretcher, the girl opened her eyes and touched Brenda's wrist. "I forgot something," she mumbled. "Have to talk to a policeman again."

"But hon, you're very weak. Can't it wait till you get to the hospital?"

"No." Tracie shook her head. "Important...Now."

Brenda turned to the EMTs. "Put her down," she ordered. "I gotta go find a cop first."

Merlynn waddled as quickly as she could through the dense shrubbery that surrounded her mansion. Her arm still hurt from the bullet that had grazed it, but she had torn off part of the bottom of her dress and used the cloth as a bandage. Her stomach and shoulder ached too from the stones the mob had flung at her. Also, she was extraordinarily hungry. It had been a long time since she had last eaten.

After having been momentarily dazed by her fall, Merlynn had lifted herself out of the bush, amazed she had suffered no additional injuries. "Maybe I can fly," she now mumbled as she continued walking through the brush. "Maybe I'm invincible, some kind of powerful new god." She chuckled, considering the idea and enjoying the countless possibilities it offered.

"Besides Merlynn, there's someone else you have to find," Tracie whispered to the detective Brenda had brought to her stretcher.

"Man who said he was the sheriff here."

"What did he look like?"

"Short, heavy, wears a cowboy hat."

"Yeah," Brenda agreed. "The same guy came into my restaurant asking lots of questions about strangers in town and got real interested when I told him about two girls visiting from New York. He wore glasses then."

The gray-mustached officer shook his head. "Still not much to go on. Anything else?"

"He drives a black SUV," Tracie said.

The policeman smirked. "Like everyone else in the county. Did he tell either of you his name?"

Brenda shook her head.

"I should've asked the guy who ran the mine," Tracie said. "But it's too late now."

"What did that sheriff have to do with all this?" the policeman asked, indicating the battle scene.

"He worked for Merlynn Baxter, and with Kimbrough dead, the sheriff's the only other person who can tell you everything that happened here." Tracie stopped talking and took a deep breath. "What she did to all the people in this town."

"Okay. We'll check it out, see if Baxter kept any records or correspondence that mention his name—phone calls, emails—and I'll send a description to the local police departments and see if maybe someone recognizes him. Any idea where this guy could be?"

"No," Tracie said. "He patrolled the whole town. He's the one who shot my friend when we switched the water in the store." She gazed into the officer's brown eyes. "Please find him," she begged softly.

Sheriff Dugan closed his eyes for a moment as he sat nervously in his parked car with Man 24 still in the front seat and the two comatose passengers in the rear. *How the hell am I gonna get outta this mess?* He had heard the blaring of the sirens and then the rumbles of the emergency vehicles as they converged on Merlynn's house.

The Ford Explorer was burrowed in the dense brush on the far side of the woman's huge property. When he'd finally been able to retrieve his phone messages, that's where Merlynn had told him to be. Even with the threat of law enforcement officers prowling nearby, he wasn't about to disobey his boss. He knew how merciless she could be.

He looked at his watch. It was already after three o'clock, well past the time she'd told him she'd be there. If she didn't arrive soon, the area would be swarming with cops. He could already hear faint sounds in the distance. "Hurry up, damn it!" he muttered.

As the medics loaded Tracie and the remaining wounded into the last ambulance, police officers stayed at the crime scene talking to the former mine workers, trying to piece together what had happened to them. It was a difficult task since the men and women who had fought with Tracie couldn't remember anything that had occurred during their prolonged trances.

"What about where you live?" one officer asked a woman who seemed to be in her mid-forties. "Can you tell me where your house is?"

"I have no idea where I've been staying," the woman said, shaking her head, her long brown ponytail swaying back and forth. "I just remember eating dinner with my husband and four-year-old daughter. But that was thirteen years ago. Please find them." She grabbed the policeman's arm and gripped it tightly.

After writing down the names of the woman, her husband, and her daughter, the officer promised to search for them. Then he turned to the next person. "Your name, please?"

A few yards away, a female officer questioned two of the

younger workers who had been part of the job force. Although the children did remember their recent lives, she was puzzled by their responses. "That's your name—Boy 11?" she asked the blond youth.

"Yes," he replied in his clipped speech. "I am Boy 11 and this is Boy 2." He pointed to the taller young teen next to him.

"Where do you both live?"

"I lived in the house with the other boys," Boy 11 said. "I went to school with them. Then I was brought here to see the bad woman. And now I do not know where I live."

"It is the same with me." Boy 2 nodded, his curly dark brown hair bobbing up and down.

"What about your parents?"

"I read about parents—mother and father," Boy 11 said. "But I do not have them. We do not have a family like in the books."

The officer gazed sadly at the two boys. "Can you tell me where your house is?" she whispered.

Merlynn struggled through the tall bushes, the pain of her wounds combined with the long trek forcing her to periodically stop and rest. As she sat quietly, breathing heavily and trying to regain her strength, she heard the faint murmur of people's voices in the distance.

"Damn!" she muttered, hoisting herself up and continuing through the shrubs, trying to walk even faster. Fortunately, she knew the quickest route to the edge of her property, adjoining another back road. "He'd better be there," she mumbled. *Hope he's got food.*

Gasping mightily, she reached the meeting place and immediately spied Dugan's black Explorer. After taking one last giant step, she flung her body against the side of the car and banged on the passenger door. "Out!" she ordered Man 24, her huge chest heaving as she uttered the word. "Sit...in...the...back."

He immediately obeyed and moved into the rear, pushing the sleeping man and woman closer together and sitting on top of the stuffed Snoopy toy, which he ignored. Merlynn, still breathing heavily and not speaking, climbed into the seat next to the sheriff.

Dugan noted her bleeding arm and bedraggled appearance. "Are you okay?" he finally asked.

"No, you idiot," she muttered. "I'm not okay. One of them shot me and others threw stones. Then someone came after me with a goddamn axe and I fell out the window. Can you believe it?" She stared at the sheriff, waiting for his reaction.

How's she still alive? he wondered. "Amazing you were able to make it all the way to the car after going through that," he said out loud. "But we should get out of here. I heard police."

"Yeah. Me too. Start driving."

"Where to?"

"Just get to 233 and go south. I'll explain the rest on the way. Right now, I'm starving. Got any food?"

Besides searching for Merlynn and Dugan, the local authorities scoured Corsonia looking for other residents. Using Boy 11's and Boy 2's clues, they were able to easily locate the boys' school. The adult supervising the six children was a robotic man who offered no resistance, but was unable to tell them anything other than his name: Man 39.

A few miles away, among abandoned houses, the police found a girls' school filled with eight young students who spoke in clipped voices, just like the boys. The woman with them was in a state of confused hysteria, unable to understand what she was doing in a school full of strange young girls who had numbers instead of names and called her "Teacher."

"I'm an accountant and I know absolutely nothing about teaching," the moonfaced brunette explained. "But these girls say

I'm their regular teacher. What's going on here? I tried to call my office, but I couldn't even find a phone."

In another house nearby, searchers discovered four young toddlers who romped in a large open room with no toys and, in the adjacent room, they found five infants who lay side-by-side in undecorated cribs, sleeping or staring at the dirty white ceiling. A zombie-like woman was in charge of the little children. As one of the officers attempted to question the scrawny gray-haired woman, a little boy in a diaper tugged wordlessly on her leg, his efforts producing no reaction.

"What's your name?" the policeman asked.

"I am Woman 35," she replied in a monotone.

"What do you do here?"

"I feed the children. I change their diapers. I put them to sleep."

"Who are the parents of these children?"

"I do not know."

The officer shook his head in frustration and after asking several other questions and getting more useless responses, he left the nursery to report what he had found.

In yet another part of Corsonia, the police discovered two dorm-like buildings with mattresses on the floor that, based on the clothing in numbered plastic carts, housed the older boys and girls. Similarly, they found several commune-style coed residences for the adults with rows of mattresses and portable numbered carts. All the living quarters were neat and clean, but contained no decorations or personal possessions.

The local authorities issued police bulletins and released descriptions of Merlynn and the sheriff that were announced on radio and posted on TV and the Internet. But the media blitz didn't produce any immediate leads. As a result, the police continued their search and questioned those Corsonia residents who were able to talk, although none of the adults could remember anything that had happened during the last thirteen plus years.

"...and the man, whose name is Thomas Dugan, may be driving a black Ford Explorer, license plate QLV6943."

Merlynn turned off the SUV's radio in disgust. "We have to ditch this car and get another one," she told the sheriff in between bites of the Snickers bar he had given her.

"How're we going to do that, especially with them in the back?" Dugan nodded toward the expressionless servant and the two comatose passengers.

"We'll keep Man 24 since he could be useful. But we'll dump the other two somewhere. When they wake up, they won't remember anything anyway."

"They'll remember me giving them the water."

"So what? The cops already know about all that and the teacher and housekeeper'll be asleep for at least another eight hours. We'll be long gone by then." She shrugged. "Of course, if you want to just kill them, we can do that too."

"No. No more killing." The sheriff glanced at Merlynn. "So how do you plan to get us another car? There's no traffic at all here."

"Just keep heading south," she said, savoring the last piece of chocolate. "We should start seeing a few cars before we hit the highway—and all we need is one. Do you still have the water in the back?"

"Yeah. Ten cases."

Merlynn chuckled. "More than enough."

The authorities found one other occupied dwelling in Corsonia—a small crafts-laden house, befitting the town's reputation as a commune. The shabby living room contained a sewing machine, two looms, skeins of wool, bolts of fabric, and other weaving and sewing supplies.

The two occupants of the house were both young women. One

was in her mid-twenties; the other was a young teenager. Each was visibly pregnant and deeply upset.

"How could this happen?" the older woman, a freckle-faced blonde asked the policeman as she stared at her bulging belly. "I was eleven-years-old, in school, living at home with my parents. I never had sex with anyone and I'm not old enough to be married." She put her head between her hands and began sobbing. "I'm just a kid. I can't be a mother." With tear-filled eyes, she looked up and wailed, "I want my mommy. Please help me!"

The officer patted her arm gently. "We're trying," he said. "Just take it easy now. Give me your name and we'll check."

"I'm Alana Ross," the woman said before bursting into tears again.

The teenager, a round-faced girl with a few pimples and curly auburn hair in a short ponytail, sat quietly, contemplating the dirty gray carpet.

"Can I have your name, please?" the policeman asked quietly.

"I am Girl 14," she whispered, slowly lifting her head.

"Do you know how you..." The officer gazed awkwardly at the young girl's face, not wanting to embarrass her.

The teen shook her head sadly. "I was in school with the other girls. Then Teacher said I would not go to school anymore. I was brought to a woman's house. She put me in a big chair and gave me water..." Girl 14 shrugged. "That is the last that I remember." She began crying softly, the tears streaming down her cheeks. "I want to be with the other girls."

Dugan drove silently on the empty road, heading toward the interstate.

"Okay," Merlynn ordered. "Stop here."

"Why? There's no other cars yet."

"I don't want to get too close to the highway. Just pull over here."

The sheriff did as he was told. "Now what?"

Merlynn turned to the back of the SUV. "Man 24, take the woman and the man next to you and put them both behind those rocks," she ordered, pointing to a clump of large stones near the road. "Tom, you help him." Then she shrugged and shook her head. "Too bad. They would have been good to keep."

As Dugan and Man 24 lifted Pamela, the sheriff noticed Snoopy on the seat. "What about this toy?" he asked. "She was carrying it."

"Toss it in with them," Merlynn said, chuckling. "It'll give her something to play with when she wakes up."

After the men finished dragging the two sleeping passengers behind the rocks, they returned to the car.

"Good," Merlynn said. "You can't see them at all from here."

"What next?" Dugan asked as he sat in the driver's seat.

"Now we wait, like we're trying to get to 80 and our car died." Merlynn looked in the rear-view mirror. "Man 24," she said. "Stand outside and as soon as you see a car in either direction, jump up and down and wave your hands to make them stop."

She turned and faced the sheriff. "Got anything else to eat?"

"Hi, honey," Brenda said as Tracie opened her eyes in her bed in Northeastern Nevada Regional Hospital in Elko. "How're you feeling?"

"Very sleepy." She blinked several times, trying to focus on the blonde waitress sitting on the chair beside her. "What happened?"

"The doctors here worked on your tummy. Cleaned it and sewed you up, they told me. You've been asleep for a while." Brenda smiled and took Tracie's limp hand. "They said you're gonna be just fine in a couple of days."

"What about Loren? What've they done with her?"

"I think they put all them robot people someplace else in the hospital. One of the cops told me they gave them pills to put them to sleep."

"Good." Tracie took a deep breath. "I can't wait to see the real Loren again."

"Yeah. The robot version hurt you pretty bad."

"That wasn't Loren."

"I know." The waitress patted Tracie's arm tenderly. "She didn't mean to do it."

"What about Matt and all the others from the mine?"

"The cops are talking to them, trying to figure out who belongs to who. What a mess!" She smiled at Tracie. "Your friend Matt told me back at the house that he wanted to visit you here, but they won't let him go till they're done with their questions."

The girl nodded. "I'd love to see him. Did they catch that woman, Merlynn, and the sheriff yet?"

Brenda shook her head slowly. "I don't think so 'cause the cops haven't said nothing and there's nothing about it on the TV. They must all be out there, still looking for them."

Tracie sighed and closed her eyes again.

About fifteen minutes after Dugan stopped the car, the first vehicle appeared, traveling in their direction. As instructed, Man 24 stepped near the road, waved his arms, and the gold Lincoln Continental stopped a few feet in front of him.

A man poked his balding gray head out of the window as Dugan hustled out of his car to talk to him.

"What's the problem?" the man asked.

"My car suddenly died," Dugan, wearing his brown wig and glasses, explained. "Don't know what's wrong with it, but we were hoping for a lift. No cell reception out here in the middle of nowhere to even call for help." He smiled at the stern-faced woman with silver-rimmed glasses who sat in the passenger seat. "Where're you folks headed?"

"We're on our way home to Deeth," the man replied. "Visited a couple of friends in Cobre. Lucky for you, 'cause there's nothin' else along this road. Bad place to be stuck. Can't have seen many cars."

"Actually, you're the first."

"The man chuckled. "I can believe that. How many people in your car?"

"Three." Dugan pointed to Man 24, who stood silently. "Him—and a real big woman."

"Well, this is a real big car," the man said, chuckling again. "You all should be able to fit in the back."

"Thanks." The sheriff tipped his hat. "Much obliged."

Tracie's eyes were closed as she lay in her hospital bed early Saturday evening, but she heard the sound of hushed voices.

"Can I talk to her?" a man whispered.

"I don't know," Brenda said quietly. "I think she's still sleeping."

"It's okay," Tracie said, opening her eyes. "I'm awake. Hi, Matt." She smiled at the bearded, longhaired young man as he approached her bed.

"I've been asking about you," Matt said, smiling.

"I told her," Brenda said. "Hey, while you two talk, I'm going to get myself something to eat." After flashing her toothy grin at Tracie, she grabbed her pocketbook and dashed out of the small room.

"So how're you doing?" Matt asked as he sat in Brenda's vacated chair and patted Tracie's arm.

"I'm okay. Mostly tired. How about you?"

"Well, I talked to the police. They're trying to figure out who everyone is and match them to who they belong with." His face brightened. "Guess what? They found my mom. She looks a lot older, but I knew who she was as soon as they brought her over to see me." He exhaled deeply. "You know what, though? She didn't know who I was at first. I guess I must look a lot different, huh?"

"Matt, you were a kid the last time she remembers and now you're all grown up."

"I don't feel like a grownup though."

"It'll take time, but you'll get there. What happened with your mom?"

"Well, as soon as I started talking to her, she got all choked up, started crying, kissing, and hugging me, yelling, 'Matty! Matty!'" He glanced at Tracie and whispered, "She hasn't called me Matty since I was a real little kid."

"What about the rest of your family?"

Matt shook his head. "The policeman told us they didn't know anything about my brother or father yet."

The man driving the Lincoln Continental stared at Merlynn's bandaged arm and tattered clothing as she struggled to fit her body into the back seat of his car. "What happened to you?" he asked.

"Oh, I had a little problem when I was taking a stroll in the woods. Cut myself when I stumbled and fell on a sharp tree branch." She smiled demurely at the man. "But, don't worry. I'm okay now, not bleeding anymore, so I won't mess up your lovely car."

Merlynn sat wedged tightly between Dugan and Man 24. A case of bottled water, salvaged from the sheriff's car before he and Man 24 had spilled out the rest, lay at their feet.

"It's starting to get dark, but it's still pretty hot out today," Dugan said, reaching for one of the bottles and unscrewing it as if he intended to take a sip. "You folks want any water?" He lifted an unopened bottle and held it in the direction of the woman in the front seat.

"Thanks," the woman said, turning toward the sheriff and nodding her head. "I could use a drink."

Dugan handed her the bottle. "How about you?" he asked the driver.

"No. I'm okay." The man turned onto the road and began driving toward Route 80.

The woman next to the driver took several large gulps of water, replaced the lid, and closed her eyes. As the bottle tumbled to the floor, her head flopped on the backrest and her glasses slid onto the floor.

"Hey, Flo," the man said. "You so tired already?"

The woman didn't answer and her body leaned awkwardly against the window.

"Okay," the driver said. "You want to sleep, go ahead. We still got time till we get home." He glanced at his passengers in the rear-view mirror. "So where were you people heading when your car broke down?"

"Elko," Merlynn lied. "We've got some business in town."

"Oh. What kind of business are you in?"

"Mining," she replied truthfully. "We operate a gold mine."

The man smiled. "Sounds like an interesting line of work. Make a lot of money?"

"We do all right," Merlynn said, returning his smile. "Sure you don't want something to drink?"

"No, thanks. I'm fine."

They drove in silence for the next several minutes until Merlynn spoke again. "I'm sorry," she said. "But I really have to go to the bathroom. Could you please stop the car for a minute?"

"Sure," the driver said, immediately pulling over to the side of the empty road.

Dugan stepped out of the car to allow Merlynn to exit. Before getting up, she whispered a few words into Man 24's ear, handed him something, and then nodded to Dugan before waddling several feet away in the twilight.

The sheriff walked next to the driver, who leaned over the comatose woman beside him, frantically trying to rouse her.

"What's wrong with my wife?" the man asked, lowering the

window. "I can't wake her up." His face was contorted with fear.

"Don't worry," the sheriff said. "She'll be okay. But I'm afraid you won't be—Man 24, now!"

From the backseat, Man 24 lunged forward and, with both hands, wrapped a long strip of Merlynn's muumuu around the elderly driver's neck, tightening the pressure until the startled man's head drooped and he fell unconscious. Man 24 held the cloth firmly around the driver's head for several additional minutes.

"That's enough," Dugan finally said. "You can let go. He's dead."

Merlynn, who had been watching the action, moved next to the sheriff. "Good work, Man 24," she said. Then she turned to Dugan. "Now you and Man 24, toss this guy's body into the bushes, away from the road, and stash Sleeping Beauty in the back seat with Man 24. Maybe we can use her. But do it fast because it's getting late and we still have a long way to go."

CHAPTER 24

Early Saturday evening, as Tracie slept in her hospital bed and Brenda sat next to her reading *People* magazine, a muscular policeman entered the room. "Excuse me," he said. "I've got some new information about the missing suspects and I hope you and Miss Martinez can help."

"Sure." Brenda lowered the magazine. "Want me to wake her?"

"If you don't mind."

"Honey," Brenda said, walking to the front of the bed and rubbing Tracie's arm lightly. "Wake up. Someone's gotta to talk to you."

Tracie opened her eyes and stared at the middle-aged uniformed man with a steel-colored crew cut. "Has something happened?" she asked.

"That guy who told you he was the sheriff, Tom Dugan, we found his abandoned Explorer on Route 233 near the highway," the policeman said. "But there was no trace of him or the Baxter woman. Since you two are the only ones here who can remember talking to him, we thought maybe you'd have some idea of where they're headed."

"You think they switched cars?" Tracie asked.

"Must have. Probably swiped another vehicle."

"Did you find any people?" the girl continued.

"Yeah, a sleeping man and woman in the woods nearby, drugged, presumably with the same water. We found cases of empty bottles in the rear of Dugan's car. But the only thing with the two people was a toy Snoopy. They didn't have IDs on them so we first have to figure out who they are before we can determine if it was their car the suspects took." He paused and glanced from Brenda to Tracie. "Do either of you remember Dugan saying anything that might help?"

Tracie shrugged. "I never had a real conversation with the sheriff. First he threatened me and my friend—and then he shot at us and captured Loren."

Brenda nodded her head several times. "I did talk to the man a little at the restaurant, and, you know, he told me he came from Wells, and I said there's an airport there, Harriet Field. Could that be important?"

The policeman smiled at her. "Yeah," he said. "It sure could."

"I'm hungry and getting real tired," Dugan said. "Let's take a little break at the next gas station—fill up the car and get something to eat."

"You're tired and hungry?" Merlynn asked incredulously. "What about me? I've been shot, hit with rocks, thrown out of a window, haven't eaten for hours—and you're the one complaining." She shook her head. "You've gotta keep driving. We should be there in about an hour."

"I don't think we have enough gas to make it." Dugan looked at the fuel gauge. "We're nearly on empty so I'm stopping at the next station." He nodded toward lights shining from the windows of a house near the road. "At least we're on the highway so there's gotta be someplace to stop."

Fifteen minutes later, he pulled into a service station with a diner next door.

"Be careful," Merlynn warned. "They're all looking for us."

"I'm putting on my glasses again and I'm already wearing the wig," Dugan said, shaking the brown hairpiece and placing his Stetson on the seat. He turned to Merlynn. "You're much easier to recognize so you'd better stay in the car."

"As long as you bring me food first. Get me four burgers, fries, a Coke, and I hope they have Hostess cupcakes. Do you have any cash 'cause they'll trace a credit card?"

Dugan opened his wallet and counted the bills. "Just two twenties and a few ones."

"That's not enough. Maybe Sleeping Beauty's got some money. Man 24, give me the woman's bag," she ordered.

The servant immediately handed Merlynn a faux leather black bag. She unfastened it, took out a pink wallet, and glanced inside. "Nah, just ten bucks. We still need more—Turn around."

As soon as Dugan looked away, she reached into her bra, removed a heavy pouch, opened it, and lifted a thick wad of money. After quickly withdrawing one bill, she again shoved the pouch inside her underwear. "Here," she said, handing the sheriff a hundred dollar bill. "This should cover everything."

Tracie waited until the beefy policeman left her hospital room. Then she grinned at Brenda. "We're going there too."

"What?"

"You heard me. He thinks they're headed to that airport so I want to go there too."

"Hon, did you somehow forget that you just got stabbed in the stomach? You're very weak. I've been sitting here watching you and you've been sleeping nearly all the time." She shook her head. "You can't leave the hospital."

"Wanna bet?" Tracie sat up, wincing slightly, and shifted her feet to the side of the bed. "Get me my clothes, please."

"What clothes? The filthy ones that are ripped and covered with blood?"

"Oh, I forgot." She thought for a moment and then smiled again at the waitress. "Hey, Brenda, I need you to do me a little favor."

The food and gas stop went smoothly and Dugan drove silently without any further interruptions. Cellophane wrappers from consumed Hostess cupcakes littered the front floor of the car as Merlynn dozed, snoring noisily and occasionally bumping into him. In the backseat, Man 24 sat at attention, staring blankly straight ahead at the road and ignoring the comatose woman sprawled next to him, her right arm dangling over his legs.

Dugan saw the sign announcing their destination and quickly roused Merlynn. "Wake up," he said. "We're here."

"I feel so much better after my little nap," she said, stretching her arms and rubbing her eyes. "Now I'm all ready for our next step." As Dugan turned off the highway into the airport entrance, Merlynn saw the runway, illuminated by floodlights, and smiled. The private twin propeller plane she had hired was sitting there, the ramp lowered, looking ready to load passengers.

As Dugan made a left and headed for the small parking lot, Merlynn stopped him. "No," she said. "Drive right next to the plane."

"I can't do that."

"Sure you can."

"Why?"

"You'll see."

When the car reached the plane, Dugan put it in Park and faced Merlynn. "Okay, " he said. "What now?"

"You shouldn't be doing this," Brenda told Tracie as the girl stepped into a pair of black jeans and zipped them.

"Yes, I should. Maybe I can help the police." The jeans were much too large for Tracie so she rolled them loosely below her waist, avoiding the bandaged wound. "Thanks for getting these for me."

Brenda snorted. "Yeah, right. Stealing them, you mean. Wonder what the lady in the room down the hall's gonna think when she gets ready to go home and finds out she's got no clothes."

Tracie lifted the pink tee shirt over her head, wincing as she moved.

Brenda noticed the girl's pained expression. "See, you're hurting already," she said. "This ain't gonna work, hon. Why don't you just go back into bed and forget this crazy idea?"

"No. This is what Loren would want me to do. It'll be okay. I'll be able to rest in the car when you're driving."

"I don't know. It's a pretty long ride, nearly an hour."

"I'll be fine," Tracie said, sitting on the bed. "Just give me my sneakers and then we can go."

The police SWAT team waited in the control tower of Harriet Field, rifles aimed at the Lincoln Continental as the car pulled up to the private plane.

"Everybody ready?" Captain Darryl Pearce asked, his large dark brown hand on the microphone. "Got the target lined up in your sights?"

A few men nodded their heads and several officers, including one young woman, mumbled assents.

As the sharpshooters watched and waited, a tall and thin bearded man with a ponytail stepped out of the backseat and, limping slightly, walked up the three-step ramp and into the plane.

"Who the hell's that?" one of the policemen asked.

"I don't know," Captain Pearce replied. "Hold your positions."

A minute later, the man returned to the car, opened the front passenger door, and reached inside. Then the driver's door opened and a short heavyset man got out, his arms wrapped around a woman whom he held high in front of him as he backed toward the plane.

"He's using her as a human shield," the captain muttered. "Can you get a clear shot?"

"Negative," one of the men replied.

The tall bearded man meanwhile extracted an obese woman whom he carefully placed behind him. The two of them each took small backward steps moving slowly toward the plane.

"That's definitely Baxter," Pearce said. "Can you shoot her behind that man? She's so damn wide."

"We can try, but it won't be very effective," the woman sniper said. "At best, we'll just graze her and we risk hitting him."

Captain Pearce shook his shiny bald head in frustration and picked up the microphone. "This is the police," he said, the words reverberating on the runway. "Surrender immediately or we will be forced to shoot!"

Brenda drove quickly along I-80, heading east from Elko. The night was clear and quiet, with just the occasional rumblings of a passing car or truck. As she had promised, Tracie leaned her head against the cushion, not talking and keeping her eyes closed during the ride. Despite her efforts to stay awake, she soon fell asleep.

Brenda turned off the highway when she saw the sign for the airport and continued toward the small main building. As she pulled into the parking lot, a police officer approached the car.

Brenda lowered her window and the man leaned inside. "Sorry, ma'am," he said. "The airport's closed tonight for official business."

Brenda glanced at Tracie, still fast asleep beside her. "Okay," she said. "When will it open?"

The officer shrugged. "I can't say."

"Any motel around here?"

"Should be one on the interstate," the man suggested. "Good luck."

Brenda nodded, closed her window, and made a U-turn. The jerky back-and-forth motion woke Tracie.

"Where are we?" the girl asked groggily.

"At the airport, but they won't let us in."

"What?" Tracie sat up quickly and then groaned in pain.

"Take it easy, hon. The airport's closed."

"Not for us. Brenda, go back."

"Honey, you're not up to doing this. Let's find a motel so you can rest tonight."

"I'll rest tomorrow. Turn around."

Brenda made another U-turn and went back to the airport.

Dugan stood uncomfortably on the tarmac, holding the comatose woman, when he heard the police announcement. "Damn," he muttered as he waited for Merlynn to position herself behind Man 24, grasp the rope, climb the steps, and board the plane.

"At least the cops aren't in here," Merlynn said as she backed inside. "That's why I had Man 24 check first. I figured they could be at the airport, but they're bluffing. They won't take a chance and shoot us with other people in the way." Dugan followed, hoisting the sleeping woman in front of him.

They entered a cabin the size of a large SUV, with two sets of comfy armchairs facing each other. To the left, an open archway housed the two-seat cockpit.

"Man 24, sit on the floor," Merlynn ordered. "Dump Sleeping Beauty in a chair and then you sit on the floor too, Tom. The cops can get a good shot at you if you're in the seat." She nodded toward the round windows. "Speaking of the cops, they must've taken the pilot. Gimme your phone."

As Dugan took out his cell, Merlynn snatched it from his hands, quickly found the number for the Harriet Field control tower, and punched it in. "Fuel this plane and send the pilot back here or we'll kill the two hostages," she said as soon as the phone was answered. "You've got ten minutes before we toss out the first body."

"Wait a sec," Captain Pearce said. "Let's talk about this. I'm sure we can work something out."

"There's nothing to work out. You either get the plane fueled and give us the pilot or we'll kill two innocent people—and I'll call the news stations first to make sure you won't be able to cover up that little detail."

"Give us the hostages and then we'll let you go."

Merlynn snorted. "Sure you will." She glanced at her watch. "Okay, now you're down to nine minutes. Better get started soon." She ended the call.

"Do you think they'll really let us fly out of here?" Dugan asked.

"They have to. They've got no other choice. The cops know I'll kill those two—and the public won't let them get away with it. Everyone hates the idea of poor innocent people dying in hostage situations like this. So tragic." She shook her head and rolled her eyes, feigning extreme sadness.

The same police officer stopped Brenda's car as she pulled into the airport's parking lot for the second time. "I just told you this airport is closed," he said, frowning when Brenda lowered her window. "Why are you here again?"

"Because maybe I can help you get Merlynn Baxter and the sheriff," Tracie said. "I'm Tracie Martinez, the one who freed the miners and attacked her house today. I know what she did to all those people and I really want her caught."

The officer nodded at Tracie. "I heard about you. Good job. Wait here and I'll see if I can get you inside."

The officer returned almost immediately. "The suspects just got into the plane," he said. "The captain says you both should come with me—quickly."

With Tracie leaning on the policeman for support, she and Brenda headed into the building. When they entered, Pearce turned away from the scene on the tarmac and stared at Tracie. "So you're the famous young lady who uncovered all this," the imposing leader said in a booming voice, his dark brown eyes fixed on the girl.

"Yes, with my friend, Loren. But what's going on?"

"The Baxter woman and Dugan are inside the plane with a couple of unidentified people and Baxter's making demands that we can't agree to," he replied, ushering Tracie and Brenda into two seats in front of the huge windowed wall facing the runway. "But not to worry. We've got a good plan of our own."

A minute after Merlynn's phone call, she and Dugan heard the sound of an approaching vehicle. Soon a fuel truck pulled up to the plane and began filling the tank.

"See," Merlynn smirked. "That's the first step."

As they peeked carefully through the bottom of the windows, a man walked toward them on the tarmac, both hands raised high above his head.

"Is that the pilot?" Dugan asked.

"I don't know. I never met the guy—just hired him over the phone. Name's Jake Ramos. You got your gun out?"

The sheriff nodded.

"Cover him as soon as he comes in."

When they heard a knock, Merlynn ordered Man 24 to release the door latch and a slightly built Hispanic man stepped into the plane, his hands still held above his head.

"What's your name?" Merlynn asked from behind Man 24, whom she had again positioned as a shield.

"Jake Ramos," the man replied, speaking with a faint Spanish accent. "You called me this afternoon to fly you to Tijuana."

"You better be the pilot or you're a dead man," she said. "Man 24, pat his body and see if he's carrying a gun."

The robotic servant did as he was ordered. "There is no gun," he said.

"Good." Merlynn turned to the pilot. "Get started—and Tom, you keep low in the seat and watch him."

The sheriff, his gun still aimed at Ramos' head, nodded, and the two men walked into the cockpit. The pilot sat and began fiddling with the control panel, moving levers and turning a few dials. Then he shook his head. "Something's wrong here. The plane doesn't feel right. Let me call another..."

"Bullshit!" Merlynn screamed. "You're not the pilot—you're a cop! Shoot...!"

Before Merlynn could finish her order, the man lunged at Dugan, knocking him against the instrument panel. The sheriff's head hit a large pointed gauge, momentarily dazing him, and the gun fell from his hand.

The pilot entered the cabin and approached Man 24, who continued to shield Merlynn.

"Hit him in the head!" she shouted.

Man 24 swung at the pilot, but he ducked and punched the servant hard in the stomach. The robotic man crumpled to the floor, his face contorted in pain.

As the pilot reached for Merlynn, she spied Dugan's gun on the floor, only a foot away. Grabbing the weapon, she aimed it at him. "Nice try, Hercules," she said, smiling. "Now before you die, which one of the hostages do you want me to kill first?"

"Shouldn't he be calling you by now if the plan worked?" Tracie asked Captain Pearce.

"It's only been five minutes," he said, checking his watch. "Meanwhile, the team's in place outside. If they see anything wrong, they'll take action."

After the officer masquerading as a pilot had entered the plane, the SWAT team crept noiselessly onto the tarmac, hiding behind the fuel truck and positioning members against the side of the plane. One sniper glanced into the window and saw the gun pointed at his comrade. "Now!" he yelled.

The SWAT squad rushed up the ramp steps and into the plane, weapons aimed.

"Not even a knock?" Merlynn asked. Her left arm was wrapped tightly around the phony pilot's neck; the right hand cocked a gun at his head. "You shoot me and your friend's a dead man."

The snipers paused, guns still pointed at Merlynn.

"Man 24, come over here and stand in front of me," she ordered.

The zombie servant obeyed and moved directly into the line of fire.

The police officers lowered their guns and remained facing Merlynn.

"That's much better," she said, smiling. "Now I want all of you to step backwards and get your asses off this plane. It's been more than ten minutes, but I'm a reasonable person. You get the real pilot on this plane within the next ten minutes, I won't kill anyone and I'll even give you a live hostage." Merlynn frowned. "That's the only deal I'm making till I get the pilot. And this time, it better be the real pilot."

"The police are backing off the plane—and Baxter and the sheriff are still inside," Tracie whispered.

Pearce was silent for a moment as he watched the scene on

the runway. "This isn't looking good," he acknowledged as his cell phone rang. He picked up the phone and listened to the caller. "Thanks," he said a minute later, frowning as he lowered the phone. "She's got Fernandez and she wants the real pilot."

"You can't do that," Tracie said.

"I know." The captain shook his head and sighed. "The pilot's too frightened anyway. He wouldn't go on that plane even if I ordered him to do it." After linking his hands behind his head, he stared at the tarmac. "So now what? We've got less than ten minutes."

Tracie gazed at him. "Maybe I have an idea."

Merlynn sat on the floor of the plane and checked her wrist. "It's almost the deadline. Do you see anything?"

Dugan, massaging his wounded forehead, crept forward and peered carefully through the bottom of a window. "Someone's walking here with his hands up."

Merlynn smiled. "This time, cover the man with your gun—and don't let him get it." She smirked at Fernandez, who also sat on the floor, securely tied to the back of the empty second row aisle seat with another piece of the bottom of her muumuu.

The policeman stared at her, but said nothing.

A knock sounded on the plane's door. "Lower the stairs," Merlynn told Man 24. "Come in with your hands up," she ordered, again sitting behind the servant as the man mounted the steps.

A fair-skinned young man with a blond crew cut entered the cabin, his hands raised.

"You can't be Ramos," Merlynn said, turning to the sheriff, who had his gun aimed at the newcomer's face. "Tom..."

"You're right," the blond man interrupted, still holding his hands over his head. "The pilot you hired is too scared to come—and that's the truth. I'm a policeman, but I'm also a pilot, the only other pilot at the airport tonight, so it's either me or nobody."

Merlynn studied the man for a moment. "Try anything and you're dead," she finally said.

The pilot nodded.

"Frisk him," Merlynn instructed Man 24. "Tell me if he's carrying a weapon."

The servant patted the man's body. "He does not have a weapon," the man said in his monotone voice.

"All right." Merlynn gave each of them orders. "Man 24, raise the ramp and then stand in front of me again." She pointed her index finger at the young policeman. "You sit down and get this plane started. Tom, crouch low on the seat next to him and keep that gun aimed at his head at all times."

"I will."

The pilot sat in the left control seat. "Before I begin, you promised to release a hostage," he said, turning around to glance at the bound policeman. "How about Fernandez?"

Merlynn smiled. "I did promise. But I get to choose. Man 24, take Sleeping Beauty and throw her off the plane. She's worthless to us right now anyway."

The servant dragged the comatose woman to the door, opened it, and tossed her onto the tarmac.

"Who's that?" Tracie asked, gazing at the motionless woman lying in a heap next to the plane.

"We don't know," Pearce replied. "But Dugan used her before as a shield to get on the plane."

"She's not moving," Brenda said. "Is she dead?"

The captain shrugged.

"Maybe not," Tracie replied. "She could've drank some of Baxter's water and is in a deep drugged kind of sleep." She turned to Pearce. "That's what happened to my friend, Loren."

The captain nodded. "Let's see what Haynes can do now," he

said. "Fernandez and that other man are still on the plane."

"Yeah," Tracie said, biting her lip.

Jason Haynes sat in front of the plane's control panel, releasing levers and setting various dials and gauges. "I'm positioning the plane for take-off," he told Merlynn, who was still on the floor of the cabin, shielded behind Man 24. "We're going to be moving so I'll need everybody seated."

Merlynn forced her large body into the right passenger seat in the first row, slunk low, and ordered Man 24 to sit in the chair next to her. The other policeman remained tethered to the seat facing them.

The pilot taxied the plane along the runway and turned it around so it faced south.

"That's a good start," Merlynn said. "At least we're heading in the right direction."

"Yep," Haynes agreed as he parked the plane, the engines still running. "Now, before we take off, I'm going to need everyone to fasten their seatbelts."

"No!" Merlynn shouted. "It won't fit around..."

As she mouthed her complaint, Dugan, sitting next to the pilot, glanced down at his seatbelt. At that moment, Haynes raised his right arm and knocked the sheriff to the floor, the gun falling from his hand onto the seat. In what seemed like one motion, the policeman grabbed both the weapon and Dugan's arm, twisting the man in front of him, gun pointed at his head. "Do anything and I'll shoot him," he said.

Merlynn lowered herself to the floor. "Man 24, come here!" she ordered. The robotic servant again positioned himself in front of her.

"I'm taking him and walking off the plane," Haynes said, backing toward the door, still firmly gripping Dugan. "You may as well surrender and come with me now because no one's flying you anywhere. You're going to be trapped."

Merlynn snorted. "No way I'm leaving this plane. And neither is your friend here." She nodded toward Fernandez, the bound police officer.

"Give it up, lady," Fernandez said. "You lose. No pilot's ever flying this turboprop. They'll just sit in the tower and wait you out. In a few hours, you'll get thirsty, hungry..."

"We'll see about that. Man 24—get him!"

As the servant lunged toward Haynes, the policeman turned the switch that lowered the door ramp, and he and Dugan tumbled onto the tarmac.

"Look!" Tracie exclaimed. "Your pilot got the sheriff out!" As she watched, Haynes rose, grabbed Dugan's arm, and pushed the shorter man toward the control building.

"Yes," Captain Pearce agreed. "Your seatbelt idea may have worked. But I don't see the Baxter woman, Fernandez, and that other man, so those three are still on the plane."

"And the plane's running," Brenda pointed out.

"That won't help Baxter," the captain said. "She doesn't have a pilot on the plane so it'll just burn fuel and, eventually, she'll be forced to give up and surrender."

Tracie turned to him. "What about the two men on the plane with her? Didn't she say she'd kill the hostages?"

"She did, but if she kills them both, she knows we'll just destroy the plane. I'm hoping she'll keep our officer, Fernandez, as a bargaining chip." He shrugged. "I don't know if we can save the other man though. In our favor, there's no food and water on the plane so we should be able to outlast her. There's nothing else we can do but wait."

Fernandez, still tied to the seat, smiled sweetly at Merlynn. "So what're you going to do now?"

She frowned at him and then glanced at the vacant pilot's seat, her grimace transforming into a grin. "You want to know what I'm going to do? But first, I made a promise. Man 24, stand up!"

The servant immediately obeyed.

Merlynn surveyed the cabin. "What can we use?" she muttered, opening a storage cabinet in the back of the plane and rummaging through it.

"Use for what?" Fernandez asked.

"You'll see. Aha! This will work." She handed a small box to Man 24. "Okay, this is what you must do," she said, purposely speaking loudly so Fernandez could hear her instructions.

"No!" he shouted. "You can't make him do that!"

"Oh yes, I can." She nodded her head.

"But why?"

"Because I made a promise and I always keep my word."

As Tracie, Brenda, and the captain watched the woman on the tarmac being lifted onto a stretcher, they saw a tall bearded man step down the ramp of the plane and head toward the terminal.

"That's not your officer, is it?" Tracie asked Pearce.

"No. It's that other man, the guy with the limp."

"She just let him go?" Brenda asked.

"Seems like it." The captain shrugged.

"That doesn't sound like something Merlynn Baxter would do," Tracie said.

The man walked quickly until he neared the crew retrieving the unconscious woman and then he abruptly stopped. As the police officers moved to intercept him, the man took something from his pocket and held it next to his jeans.

"He set himself on fire!" Brenda yelled.

The police tried to grab the man, but as flames encompassed his legs, he calmly lit a second match and ignited his shirt. While the people on the runway and in the control tower watched helplessly, Man 24 crumpled to the ground, his body ablaze in a white and yellow inferno.

Merlynn turned to her remaining hostage and smiled. "You asked what I'm going to do now. Here's the answer: I'm going to fly this plane."

"What?" the officer yelled. "You're not a pilot!"

"Maybe not. But I've been on turboprops before and watched what the pilot did and I'm a very fast learner." After raising the ramp and closing the door, she waddled to the control area, wriggled her way through the narrow opening, and wedged herself into the pilot's seat.

"Lady, you're crazy! Don't do this. Just give up and walk off the plane before you kill us both."

"You don't know who I am. Earlier today, I found out that I can fly."

Fernandez was too dumbfounded to speak.

"Really," Merlynn continued. "I fell out of a high window and landed on the ground with hardly a scratch. I'm like Superman—invincible—some kind of new-age goddess."

The man gazed at her sadly through the opening to the cockpit. *"Dios te salve, Maria,"* he murmured, bowing his head in prayer.

"You'll see." She released the brakes and unlatched the levers she'd seen the pilot use earlier and the plane shot forward. "Now if I do this, we should go faster," she said, pushing the two throttle-position levers further forward. The engine condition system kicked in and the turboprop raced along the runway, picking up speed. Slowly, Merlynn pulled back on the control wheel until the aircraft lifted off into the nighttime sky.

"What the...?" Captain Pearce followed the plane's ascent and nearly fell backwards.

"She's not a pilot, is she?" Tracie asked.

"We didn't think so."

"Then how...?" Tracie said, but stopped talking as she watched the plane fly gracefully in the sky. Soon it was out of their sight.

"Can we see the plane somewhere else here?" she asked.

"There're windows on the other side of the building," the captain said, moving into the hallway and opening a door.

Brenda helped Tracie walk as they followed him into a small office.

"This is great!" Merlynn exclaimed. "What awesome power an airplane has!"

"You don't know how to fly it or land."

"I'll figure it out. Let me take a look." She examined the control panel. "This is easy. If I just push this wheel forward a little..." The plane dropped a bit lower. "See?"

"Listen to me, please. At least turn on the radio and let them tell you how to fly this plane."

"No way. I can do it all myself. I want to make sure we're still going south." She studied the flight screen map on the control panel.

Fernandez glanced outside and saw an outcropping of white reflected against the black sky. "You're heading right into the mountains!" he shouted. "Lift the plane higher—now!"

"Okay. Take it easy." She grasped the control wheel and quickly pulled it toward her body. "This should work."

The plane shot upward. But, as it gained altitude, the left wing clipped a small edge of the jutting rock.

"No-o-o!" Merlynn shrieked as the speeding craft crashed heavily into the stone cliff. A thunderous noise disrupted the silent night and the plane disintegrated into thousands of shattered pieces.

EPILOGUE

Three months later
Nevada

"It feels so strange to be back here," Tracie said to Loren as they stood near the entrance of the Corsonia mine, surrounded by three enormous haul trucks.

"Yeah," Loren agreed. "But as visitors this time, not spies."

It was Saturday of the Columbus Day holiday weekend, the girls' first trip to Nevada since their July vacation, which had resulted in the town's freedom from Merlynn.

Matt—now clean-shaven, shorthaired, and much younger looking—walked over to them holding two bottles of water. "These are safe to drink," he said, smiling as he handed a bottle to each girl and then put his arm around Tracie. "So have you two seen enough here or do you want to take a look inside?"

"Nah," Tracie said, taking a sip of water. "In my one day working in the mine, I decided that's not the career choice for me."

"Me neither." Loren made a face and shook her head.

Although it had been only a few months since the girls had seen the mine, the complex already looked remarkably different. Thanks to the new ownership, modernization was well underway. Lance Kimbrough's house had been transformed into an administration building and the other century-old structures were either being replaced or updated, all construction following safety and environmental regulations. Technological advances were also being incorporated: A powerful air conditioning system and a new elevator had been installed in the shaft and the mine now included bathroom facilities.

"No more potty mine cars," Loren had said, chuckling at the memory.

The bank accounts of Merlynn, Dugan, and Kimbrough had been confiscated and the money added to the net worth of the Corsonia Gold Mine. Since the mine, valued at $145 million, was now jointly owned by the 139 surviving people of the town, each resident became an instant millionaire. The new crew of workers and geologists who labored in the complex were all paid fair wages. Understandably, none of Merlynn's miners had any desire to return to their former "jobs."

Although the residents were now wealthy, they still suffered the emotional aftereffects of more than thirteen years under Merlynn's control. When the authorities had been able to question all the survivors, they reunited as many families as they could. Unfortunately, however, most of the town's families were no longer intact.

Those who rejoined their loved ones included Matt's father and Bill and Briana Chilvers, husband and older daughter of Pamela, the boys' school housekeeper, formerly known as Woman 28. Although Arthur Slayton, the boys' teacher, found his Montello fiancée, she had given up on him many years ago and married another man.

To avoid the death penalty, "Sheriff" Thomas Dugan told the FBI interrogators, who had taken over the case, everything he knew.

"How did Merlynn Baxter do it?" they had asked. "How did she gain control of all the people?"

"She was real smart—and real patient," he had explained. "She pretended to be a new drink company and sent out free water, or soda, or juice, only to one or two families at a time at first. She made her formula weaker so, after the people drank, they fell asleep slower. But it worked the same. In the middle of the night, when the people were in a deep sleep, we'd go to their homes and she'd give them more bottles of her water and instructions. In the beginning, she just told them to drink the water every day and act the same as always, and if anyone asked about the free drinks to say that they tasted great, and wait to hear from her again."

"Weren't there any problems—like if someone didn't drink the stuff?"

Dugan had shrugged. "There was a couple of times like that. One night, we got to the house and found a scared teenage boy who tried to beat us up."

"What did you do?"

"Forced him to drink the soda and then took him back to Merlynn's house to be programmed."

"Any other incidents?"

"Once a woman called the police station all upset." Dugan had stopped talking and stared at the floor.

"And?" the FBI agent had prodded.

"Merlynn took care of the police chief in the very beginning so he came over and handled the woman, made her drink the bottle, and then called us." Dugan had lifted his head. "After a few weeks, everyone in the town belonged to her."

Other revelations from Dugan were much more horrific. When Merlynn had taken full control of the people, she had employed a Nazi-like selection process, killing any residents she deemed useless.

By her definition, "useless" included all children between the ages of two and ten because the powerful drug would devastate their small bodies and, even if they survived, children—like everyone else—couldn't learn new skills after being programmed; people over age sixty because they were too old and inefficient for arduous mine labor; and anyone who was physically or mentally disabled. Afterwards, she had continued to destroy people who developed conditions that left them unable to perform their assigned duties, including those who were maimed by her failed drug experiments.

When the FBI had asked who had carried out the murders, Dugan had whispered, "Merlynn just ordered them to kill themselves or to kill someone else. She told them how to do it— strangle, stab, shoot. And most times she watched like it was some sort of show. I tried to stop her, but..." He had covered his head with his hands and continued tearfully, "I'm so sorry I ever got started with her."

Dugan had led the authorities to the burial ground on a distant hill and they had unearthed 43 bodies. When the skeletons had been identified, they had included Matt's younger brother and Crystal, the five-year-old daughter of Pamela, the boys' school housekeeper.

Placing the new generation of children, all of whom had grown up under Merlynn's control, into traditional families proved much more difficult than reuniting existing families. None of the boys and girls had any relationship with their biological parents and the unwitting parents had no recollections of conceiving children. They had been ordered by Merlynn to have sex to procreate, much like farm animals. Moreover, the children they produced had no concept of the family structure, having been raised with each other in orphanage-like settings.

After the authorities matched DNA to determine fathers, mothers, and children, psychologists were brought in to counsel the new "families." But for most of the biologically connected couples, the process didn't work. The men and women didn't remember one another and, in several cases, didn't even like each other. That had been the situation with Pamela's surviving daughter, Briana, now the 24-year-old mother of a five-year-old son, the result of a forced encounter with an unknown partner. The little boy had been placed in a foster home while Briana remained with her mother and father, trying to come to terms with what had happened to her.

However, some of the adults did bond with each other, or with the children they had unknowingly and unwillingly created, and several new families were formed.

"Boy 11!" Tracie shouted, waving to the blond boy as he opened the door of the small white house and walked toward her and Loren.

"How are you?" Loren asked, reaching out to touch his hand.

The boy flinched slightly, but didn't pull his hand away. "I am fine," he said, his speech not nearly as stilted as it had been. "But I have a new name. I am Robert Prescott."

"Good to meet you, Robert," Tracie said, holding out her hand. "Who are you living with now?"

Robert shook Tracie's hand. "I have a mother. Her name is Margaret. And I have a little sister. She was called Girl 4, but now her name is Ella." He smiled at them. "It is like the book you gave me. I have a family."

"Do you have a father who lives with you too?" Loren asked.

He shook his head. "The man who is my father did not want to be with us. Neither did Ella's father. But there are many families without fathers. Right?"

"Yup," Tracie agreed. "Your family sounds great, Robert. We're so happy for you. How about Boy 12? Did he find his family too?"

Robert stared at the ground and shuffled his feet. "He is called Daniel and his mother and father did not want to be with him. He is living with some of the other boys like we did before." Robert gazed at the girls sadly. "Daniel is not lucky like me."

Tracie and Loren lifted their luggage out of Brenda Hartwig's trunk in front of the entrance to Elko Regional Airport's chalet-like terminal building.

"Thanks so much for letting us stay with you," Tracie said, hugging the waitress.

"My pleasure and good to see you both in such great shape after what happened." Brenda returned Tracie's hug, wrapped her arms around Loren, and smiled at the girls. "Just call me anytime you want to visit New Hope." The surviving residents of Corsonia had decided to give their notorious town a new, more appropriate, name.

"We will," Loren said.

The girls wheeled their carry-ons through the door and got on line.

"You're not leaving without saying goodbye to me, are you?" a male voice behind them asked.

"Matt!" Tracie exclaimed. She turned, he grasped her tightly, and they shared a lengthy, passionate kiss.

"Ahem," Loren finally said, clearing her throat. "The line is moving."

"So sorry." Matt smiled at Loren, not looking at all sorry. "I didn't mean to hold up the line."

"Oh yes, you did!" Tracie punched him playfully in his lean stomach. "Call me and text me," she whispered, caressing his hand.

"You know I will," he murmured. Then, nodding to Loren, he waved and left the terminal.

"So is it serious between you two?" Loren asked.

"Maybe. But not for a while. Matt's still got a lot of catching up to do. Remember, though he's twenty-four, his mind is just eleven-years-old. They're giving him and the others special school and social coaching, but he's still kinda like a horny pre-teen boy with a crush on an older girl."

"I don't know." Loren shook her head. "Looked to me like he's catching up real fast."

Tracie smiled.

The girls got their boarding passes and sat in the concourse area to wait for their respective connecting flights back to college. They attended different schools. Loren, who had enough money to enroll in even the most expensive college, was a freshman at California's Stanford University; Tracie, who had taken a student loan, attended a more affordable New York state school, SUNY Stony Brook, near her Long Island home.

Although they were still good friends, the relationship between Loren and Tracie had changed since their summer adventure. Tracie's "secret"—that Loren's mother had paid her—was not a factor. Loren had known about the arrangement from the start and didn't care.

But Tracie was different now. Being a successful leader had given her newfound confidence and she no longer deferred to Loren's steady stream of commands. Tracie now felt she had a purpose to her life. She had relished the crime-fighting experience and intended to major in criminal justice. She had even written to Captain Pearce, explaining her decision and he had responded with a promise to support and sponsor her. "You can work for me anytime," the SWAT team leader had written.

Loren heard the announcement for her flight to Reno. "Take care, Trace," she said, standing and hugging her friend warmly.

"You too." Tracie pulled away and smiled at Loren. "We did good."

Washington, D.C.

Colonel Elmer Chou finished rereading the pile of papers on his desk and then carefully placed the sheets into a file marked "Top Secret." Holding the folder securely with his left hand, the slightly built gray-haired man marched down the hall and opened the door of a small laboratory. "I'm good with everything on my end," he said to the attractive young woman seated in front of a computer. "How are you doing, Amber?"

Captain Amber Hertzberg picked up a test tube filled with a clear liquid and smiled at her superior officer. "Everything's fine, sir. I just want to test the formula on human subjects one last time. But I'm sure it will work. It always does." She gazed lovingly at the vial. "This mind-control cocktail is really awesome stuff. Lucky for us, Merlynn Baxter was a true chemical genius."

"And lucky for us, she didn't destroy her work and it wasn't ruined in that battle last summer," Colonel Chou added. "She left us everything we needed—her research, her formulas, her findings. So you're sure you'll be finished in time for our Wednesday morning meeting?"

"Definitely, sir."

"Good. You know, the general's very excited about this project."

"He should be, sir," Amber said, smiling as she twirled the test tube in her right hand. "It's all ready for our soldiers to use."

AFTERWORD

Although *Corsonia* is a work of fiction, most of the mind-control drug data included in the novel is true. The Freedom of Information Act lists about 700 mind-altering drugs, many of which can be mixed and matched to produce even more frightening combinations. Plants with powerful psychotic properties, like the zombi cucumber that fascinated Merlynn, are also real.

Fortunately, however, Merlynn's mind-control formula does not exist and, hopefully, no evil genius will ever concoct such a potent and horrifying weapon.

THE MAN
BETWEEN

AN INTERNATIONAL ROMANCE

AMELIA E. BARR

1st WORLD
LIBRARY
Literary Society

The Man Between

Amelia E. Barr

© 1st World Library, 2007
PO Box 2211
Fairfield, IA 52556
www.1stworldlibrary.com
First Edition

LCCN: 2007935433

Softcover ISBN: 978-1-4218-9304-4
Hardcover ISBN: 978-1-4218-9404-1
eBook ISBN: 978-1-4218-9204-7

Purchase *"The Man Between"*
as a traditional bound book at:
www.1stWorldLibrary.com/purchase.asp?ISBN=978-1-4218-9304-4

1st World Library is a literary, educational organization
dedicated to:

- Creating a free internet library of downloadable ebooks

- Hosting writing competitions and offering book publishing
scholarships.

Interested in more 1st World Library books? contact:
literacy@1stworldlibrary.com
Check us out at: www.1stworldlibrary.com